W9-BDX-875

31945

SHARLA

BUDGE WILSON
SHARLA

Stoddart Kids

*We acknowledge the Canada Council for the Arts and the
Ontario Arts Council for their support of our publishing program.*

Published in Canada in 1997 by Stoddart Kids,
a division of Stoddart Publishing Co. Limited
34 Lesmill Road
Toronto, Canada M3B 2T6
Tel (416) 445-3333 FAX (416)445-5967
e-mail Customer.Service@ccmailgw.genpub.com

Published in the United States in 1998 by Stoddart Kids
85 River Rock Drive, Suite 202
Buffalo, New York 14207
Toll free 1-800-805-1083
e-mail gdsinc@genpub.com

Canadian Cataloguing in Publication Data
Wilson, Budge
  Sharla

ISBN: 0-7736-7467-5

I. Title.

PS8595.I5813S57 1997   jC813'.54   C97-930669-8
PZ7.W54Sh   1997

Cover illustration: Ron Lightburn
Cover design: Tannice Goddard

Printed and bound in Canada

Acknowledgments

I would like to thank the following:

— *The Canada Council for a Short Term Grant awarded in 1994 and generously deferred until 1995, after I discovered that I could not obtain accommodation in Churchill in 1994 for the days leading up to and following Halloween.*

— *Susan Postin, who was my guide and hostess when I first visited Churchill during Children's Book Week in 1987.*

— *The students and staff of Duke of Marlborough School.*

— *Juliette Lee, the Chief Librarian of the Churchill Library, who was helpful and hospitable during both my visits to Churchill.*

— *Iva Chomyn of Churchill's Outreach Services, who gave me invaluable information and advice during and after my 1995 visit to Churchill.*

— *Laurie Gagnon of the Tundra Inn, who offered me accommodation in her own home, when it looked as though there would be no room available in Churchill for the period of time when I needed it in 1995. (People often book rooms over two years in advance of each polar bear season.)*

— *My husband, Alan Wilson, who accompanied me to Churchill and helped with the research for the book, as well as braving the high winds and numbing cold of Halloween night.*

— *Sheila Dalton, always a talented and insightful editor.*

— Leona Trainer and Kathryn Cole of Stoddart Kids.

— Sharla Russell, a grade 11 student who showed me great kindness when I was stranded in Mary's Harbour, Labrador, in 1995, when my plane could not locate its destination of Black Tickle in the fog. She has provided the name for this book's heroine.

— The many powerful and graceful polar bears that I was fortunate enough to see in their natural habitat.

****

I've taken a few liberties with plane schedules, but I hope the people of Churchill won't hold that against me. Otherwise, I've tried to be as accurate as possible in my use of Churchill as the background of this story.

This book is for Alan,
who shared the bears with me.

CHAPTER ONE

Sharla Dunfield listens to the sound of the wind in the chimney — a fierce, hollow growl. She hears the rattle of the windows, the thrum of the wooden skirt around the base of the small house. There are no trees out there to break up the sound, and the deep howl of the wind as it slams against the sides of buildings and vans seems to be the constant background music of this awful place. She looks out the window. Yes, it's snowing.

She thinks about the walk to school. Nothing is very far from anything else in

Churchill, but five blocks can seem like five miles as you struggle against the wind, so cold it feels like needles in your face. With snow, it can be a lot worse. They don't manufacture snowflakes in this town. They make grains of snow, and they don't come down; they come at you sideways. She looks at the calendar. It's October 25th. She heard someone in the Complex remark, just last night, that this was such a warm October. Warm. She thinks about January with something like fear. She is also remembering Ottawa, where she lived until three months ago. Everyone said that Ottawa was cold in the winter — colder even than Moscow — but whoever said this obviously didn't understand the true meaning of cold. Ottawa was trees, historic buildings, a beautiful canal, hills for skiing, and a lot of shopping malls. And nobody telling you to be careful where you walked because of the polar bears.

If the people here are so afraid of polar bears, why did they build the Churchill Town Centre — "The Complex" — right on the shores of Hudson Bay? That's exactly where they say the bears sometimes like to walk in late October and early November, while they're waiting for the Bay to freeze over — so they can move out onto the ice and hunt for seals. That's what they say. Sharla's never seen even one. The Bear Alert signs were put up along the beach and rocky shores in mid-September, to warn people away. *Polar Bear Alert* the signs say. Underneath that, there's a big ugly-looking black paw print. Then: *Stop. Don't walk in this area.* But Sharla figures the town councillors just posted those signs to impress the tourists.

The tourists have already filled up all the hotels, and are even spilling over into spare rooms in some of the private homes. They wander through the town with their binoculars and cameras strung around their necks, going from one craft store to another, searching for one of the few restaurants, waiting for the next Tundra Buggy to take them far out onto the tundra, where the bears *really* are.

Sharla looks upon the tourists with scorn. They're just playing. She's for real, but they

3

aren't. They have all this money (no one without a pocketful of cash can travel up here and go out on those tours), and they can hardly wait to spend it on Inuit carvings, appliqued wall-hangings, and yet another meal of Arctic char. She hates them as they trudge by in those stupid expensive leather jackets — which are useless for protecting their knees — with toques squashed down on their heads, but with their ears exposed, waiting to drop right off from frostbite. Just wait. They'll find out. They'll soon see where all that money is going to take them. Right into Emergency at the hospital, so they can discover the best way to thaw out whatever part of them has been frozen. They wear gloves so that they can do fancy finger work with their cameras. What idiots. Mitts are the only things that can save your hands in Churchill. They'll get wise soon enough. Then they can mush it over to the Arctic Trading Company to spend some more of their big money on expensive embroidered parkas and fur-lined mittens. And scarves to tie across their faces.

"Sharla!" Her mother's voice rises up the narrow stairway to shock her out of her thoughts. "You'll be late for school again if you don't hurry up! You know what Mrs. Hendrickson said last week. You're going to end up in the principal's office if you don't watch out!"

I know, I know, I know, I know. Sharla doesn't answer.

"Sharla! Did you hear me?"

"Yes, Mother. How could I help it? They must have heard you in Winnipeg."

"Well, then, *answer* me when I talk to you. And hurry! Benjamin went off in the school bus five minutes ago!"

Benjamin is nine years old, and doesn't do anything wrong. Sharla wants to aim her math book at that frosted window and pitch the damned thing right through it. Math. Another thing that's messing up her life. And why hurry? So that she can get to school in time for Miss Hendrickson to chew her out for not finishing her math homework? No way! She pulls her warm sweater on over her T-shirt, purposely taking her time. What's so scary about the principal? He can't be any worse than Mrs. Joyce or Mr. Lovitt (love it!) and Miss Hendrickson. Sometimes it seems to Sharla that the only person in the world who thinks she's great is the basketball coach, Mr. Kent. Well — she likes basketball. She's also good at it. And Mr. Kent is her hero. She stops dressing, puts her head back against the wall, and closes her eyes. Red hair, really wild. Muscles. Kind eyes.

Why can't parents be like that? Why are parents always directing and advising and scolding and nagging? Did they ever have kind eyes, way back in the dark ages when they were young? Mr. Kent is only about twenty-six. Ten years older than she is. Ten years and a bit. He isn't even over the hill. Thirty is when you're really over the hill.

Sharla clatters down the stairs and heads straight for the back porch. Boots, parka, mitts, scarf. She begins to put them all on.

"Sharla!" Her mother again. "You haven't had your breakfast!"

"No time," mumbles Sharla, as she hauls

on her boots. "I'm late. You said so yourself. I don't need any food. I'm not hungry. I'm gone. See you later."

She turns around briefly before she opens up the back door. She was right. No kind eyes in that kitchen. Her father's eyes look angry, but that's nothing new; her mother's look worried. But neither pair looks like anything you'd describe as kind.

CHAPTER TWO

Sharla stands on the back steps and surveys the scene. It looks like a frozen desert to her, with box-like houses strung out among the snowdrifts. Colorless, black and white, like an old movie. When she turns the corner onto James Street and then heads up La Verendrye Avenue towards the school, the snow is hitting her full in the face. Somewhere, way over to the right, is Hudson Bay, but because it's not visible from here, she barely glances in that direction. She knows that the waves must be crashing on the beach behind the Complex, large and fierce, with spray flying up into the air. She likes this. Mr. Kent and basketball and the pounding surf are things she's able to like. On a stormy day (and it seems to her that most of the days are stormy), the Bay speaks to something in her — the part that's so angry. All that splash and roar of waves has a way of loosening the knot in her chest that usually feels so tight and frozen.

Often, even at lunch time, she goes over to the Complex and stands in front of the big window above the beach, watching the surf. By the time she returns to school, she thinks she might possibly survive another session of algebra or geometry with Miss Hendrickson. Or the endless procession of kings and queens and politicians and wars that come her way in social studies classes, compliments of the cranky Mr. Lovitt. Well — he isn't cranky with everyone. Just with the kids he says are "unmotivated" or else have no brains. She isn't sure which category he thinks she belongs in. She knows she has plenty of brains — she was a real whiz back there in Ottawa — but why use your brains if the teacher doesn't make anything interesting? Mr. Lovitt adores battles and dates and constitutions, and he bobs his little round bald head up and down with enthusiasm when he's talking about them. She often feels mad enough to hit him. *Tell me about something fascinating, and you can bob all you like.*

It isn't just Mr. Lovitt who can't reach her. Sharla feels full of an ugly silent laughter when Mrs. Joyce quotes Tennyson or Wordsworth in her dramatic quavery voice. You can tell she's madly in love with those two poets, who always seem to be writing about heroic deeds or else daffodils and nature.

Just let those dumb poets come up here and see what they can find to write about. Maybe Tennyson could put together a long poem about her father and his lost job in Ottawa, where he'd been a big-time executive guy in a plastics firm, until the company started trying to beat the recession by laying people off, big and little, high and low. Or a heroic poem about the phony "party" and the skimpy "severance package." Severance package. What a joke. It's what they give you to make you forget the fact that you've been fired. And how would Tennyson handle the way her dad couldn't seem to find a buyer for his castle — their big house on The Driveway? And the bumpy train ride to Churchill to take a new job that he doesn't like. Or the move into a house so small that it makes the old one seem like a palace. With a skirt around the bottom, where the house was lifted up clear of the permafrost — a skirt to keep out the ever-present, ever-howling wind. Plus, how would Tennyson describe a man who seems to have forgotten how to smile?

And what about Wordsworth, with his "host of golden daffodils"? Let him try to describe a town with almost no grass, and only a few spindly, one-sided trees that have been growing for over a hundred years, but are still only about five feet tall. Of course he'd love to write about the damn polar bears (because they're a part of nature) — if he ever got a chance to see them.

Polar bears, polar bears. Sharla is sick of hearing about them. She hates the huge sculpted bear that looms over the library from his wide perch on the top shelf, not to mention the giant wooden bear outside the Complex cafeteria — the "Launching Pad" — about fifteen feet tall, with a slide inside it. The little kids climb up one end, and slide right through the bear to the other end. Great, if you're seven years old. Useless, if you're fifteen. Bears. And all those dumb tourists, with their billion-dollar cameras, coming all the way up here (voluntarily) to see if they can catch a glimpse of one. Even hiring helicopters (at hundreds of dollars an hour) to make sure they'll see a whole bunch of them.

Sharla clumps along in her heavy boots, bucking the wind, her face lost behind her long woolen scarf. She thinks about how, in Ottawa, she used to spend half-an-hour in the morning fixing her long, straight, honey-colored hair, and getting her eye make-up on just right. Then, sailing off to school without a hat, so that she could show off how great she looked. No chance of that here. She'd freeze to death if she didn't cover up every single piece of herself except her eyes. She tries not to think about other Ottawa things: all the trips the family took — even to Florida in March breaks; the zillions of times they ate in restaurants; her father's loud guffaws during the weekly poker games; the way their money seemed to be coming out of a tap that was never turned off.

Sharla decides to go past the school entrance and beyond the Complex, to have a good look at the Bay. Her mother may mind if she's late, but she couldn't care less. *As a matter of fact, I don't care about much of anything.* As she comes abreast of the road leading to the beach, she passes one of the tourists. She can tell he's a tourist by his look. They all tend to look bewildered and thrilled — and of course cold, because they're nearly always wearing the wrong clothes. Well, so many of them come from places like California or Germany or Japan, that you can't expect them to know about the Churchill wind. This one is standing in the middle of the road, fiddling with his camera, and gazing at the angry waves on the Bay. Well, she can relate to that. He's probably trying to decide whether or not he'll ignore the Bear Alert signs and go have a stroll on the frigid beach. He turns her way and says, "Hi." She grunts something from behind her scarf. Red toque. Exposed ears. Short jacket. She turns around and goes back to the entrance, but has an uneasy feeling he's still watching her.

Inside, the school is warm and bright. Something in Sharla wants to feel good about that. Something else won't let it happen. She's late, of course, and that doesn't help. But she perks up during a spare, when she sees Collette coming down the hall. She always feels comfortable enough with Collette to be exactly who she really and truly is.

"How's things?" Collette has her cheerful morning face on, and she's looking like her Cree mother today. Her father is French, from Quebec. "Ça va?"

"Ça va," replies Sharla. "Or more or less.

If you don't count crabby mothers and inhuman winds. See any bears lately?" Sharla curls her lip.

"No. But honest, Sharla, two of them came to town last October, and just sauntered up Button Street as though they owned it. At night. Before the snow came. They were so huge, and all white against the blackness of the street. I was visiting a friend over there. I saw them."

"Huh," says Sharla.

"Lookit," says Collette, "if you ever see one, just once, you'll stop being so snobby about them. You'll fall in love, just like the rest of us." She laughs.

Sharla smiles. Maybe it's true. But not likely.

But Collette hasn't finished. "You'll be so thrilled that you'll run up to the second floor of the Complex and throw yourself down the big bear slide." Then, "Your mother bugging you again?"

Sharla casts her eyes to the ceiling. "So what else is new?" she says. "Bugging me about being late for school. Telling me I'll die of starvation if I don't eat my breakfast. I don't need breakfast. Can't she realize that?"

"Well . . ." Collette speaks slowly. "I can't see how all that makes her especially awful. Most of us have mothers who bug us about being late and eating our meals. It's just a sort of normal mother thing."

"Well, maybe," says Sharla, "but Mom seems to be so worried and kind of frozen all the time. It's been like that ever since Dad lost his job and had to come up here to do something he doesn't like doing. He's used to working with his mind instead of his body. And he's an old man. He's forty-three — too old for all that lifting and shoving down at the store. It's like he's shrunk down to nothing. I don't mean his body. His spirit is all shrivelled up like a prune. And it seems like he's either mad or sad all the time. He only gets lit up when he talks about the old days in Ottawa. I don't even think he likes who he is any more."

Sharla throws back her head and sighs. Then she goes on, "So Mom's a wreck. I think she's scared he'll slip right over the edge and have some sort of breakdown. Or maybe he's in the middle of one right now. She doesn't say so, but it doesn't take a very big brain to see what's bothering her. That and money. Not having enough of it. So now both of them have developed short fuses. Step out of line one smidgen, and they're on your case. I hate that."

Collette looks hard at Sharla. "It doesn't sound like fun city," she admits. "But my dad's job is all physical stuff, and he seems to like it. Says it keeps him in shape. Maybe your dad'll get used to it. And forty-three isn't that old. Hey! There's the bell!"

Almost against her will, Sharla comes up with most of the right answers in math during the next period. Miss Hendrickson is actually smiling. Her long face looks almost soft and pleasant as she says, "Good, Sharla. I knew you could do it if you tried." *Oh, great. Be sure to tack an insult onto your compliment.* Sharla keeps her eyes down on her desk and doesn't smile back.

After the last class of the morning, Theo Hogan steps between Collette and Sharla, and turning his back on Collette, says, "Going to the movies tonight?"

"No," says Sharla. How can she tell him she doesn't have the money?

"It's a good one. I could pick you up in my dad's truck. Keep you safe from the bears." He laughs.

"No," she says. Not "No thanks." Just "No."

He shrugs his shoulders and moves away. Sharla watches him go. He's tall, with long arms and legs, a mop of unruly sandy hair, and a friendly face. She often notices him staring at her from afar. She frowns. *Why did I do that? I could have smiled or something.* Sometimes she can't figure out her reactions to things. Theo's a nice guy. She's seen him with the other kids. He has a good sense of humor and he seems to be fun to be with. When she did the conservation project with him, he really respected her input. And he likes her. She can tell. For one thing, he has kind eyes — eyes with something else in them, too. Worry, maybe. Something she can't quite figure out. She noticed it a couple of times when she let fly at him when they were working on the project. She can't even remember what made her mad. Maybe he was making too many suggestions. It certainly wasn't because he did anything dumb. He's too smart for that.

So why am I so strung up with fury? It isn't Theo's fault that my life is such a disaster. But he likes Churchill. He likes it a lot. She's overheard him say so, loads of times. How could he ever understand the way she feels about this godforsaken town? Or what it's like to be so unhappy?

Collette turns to her. "You're so dumb," she says, "that sometimes I don't understand why your head hasn't fallen off your neck. All the girls in grade eleven are chewing their nails, hoping that maybe Theo'll just smile at them. And you act like he's your own personal soccer ball to kick around. Sometimes I just don't understand what makes your wheels spin."

"Me neither," says Sharla, in a whisper. *Maybe, if I can ever get my courage up, I'll go over to the Outreach Services and see if they can tell me about my wheels.* Outreach is in the Health Centre part of the Complex, and she knows that a lot of people go there when their lives get too tangled up. But she'd feel ashamed to go. It seems to her that the people who end up there are often pregnant, or beaten up by their parents, or feeling suicidal about something or other. She's heard the other kids talking about it. No. She doesn't want to be part of that messed-up bunch. If anyone is going to straighten her out, it has to be her. Sharla Dunfield herself.

CHAPTER THREE

In the afternoon, Sharla walks over to the central part of the Complex to check out the view. But first she goes down to the library to return a book. Mrs. Cole is there, briskly going about her business, checking books out, replenishing shelves, always ready with a smile for her clients, old and young. "Hello, Sharla," she says. "Anything you'd like to borrow?"

Sharla finds herself thinking — That's one good thing about a small place — everyone knows you. Then she quickly changes tracks. *And bad, too. Nowhere to hide. Everyone familiar with your own private life.* For instance, the whole town knows that her father was fired and that he doesn't like his new job, and that her mother is looking for some kind of employment to puff out his small salary. She sighs. "No thanks, Mrs. Cole." *At least I thanked her. Not like this morning with Theo.*

Up in the wide foyer above the library, she passes the long row of photographs of former citizens of the area. She often looks at those pictures and wonders about the people in them. Some look sad or grim, others happy and sort of proud. What were they really feeling? And why? She's heard that until the 1970s there was no insulation in the houses and no running water. So what was *that* like, during the long dreary winter months? She can hardly bear to think about it. How on earth could those people have felt either happy or proud?

Today, Sharla doesn't pause to study the pictures, but walks right over to the long window and looks out. Yes, the waves are huge, riled up by the savage wind, and are pounding against the rocks with a kind of rage. The tide is rising. She loves all that fury.

It was a Monday when he came home two hours early, at four o'clock, and told us. I'll never forget the look on his face. If someone had mugged him on the way home, he wouldn't have looked more wounded, more bruised. Mom said, "What is it, Gordon?" He didn't answer her. He just sat down on the nearest chair and said over and over again in that awful dead voice, "I don't believe it. I don't believe it." It was like a funeral chant. And then he said, "All those years." Finally he buried his face in his hands, mumbling, "And I haven't saved a penny."

Sharla watches the waves for a long time. Then she sees that there is a man down there. And yes, he's that same tourist she saw yesterday in his red toque and short jacket. He's walking along the beach area — beyond the Bear Alert sign, close to the water. He raises one of his cameras and aims it directly into the surf. Better watch those tides, she thinks, talking to him in her head. They come in fast, and the difference between high and low is seventeen feet. *Vertical* feet. But she also admires the courage or recklessness that has taken him down to that forbidden area where bears can walk or hide. *Or so they say.* If it's true, why does no one ever mention seeing a bear? You'd think that during the last three long months she'd have seen at least *one*, if they were *really* nearby. She watches as the tourist gazes around a bit more — even looks up at the window — and then walks away from the area.

Far to the left, Sharla can see what looks like a shining skin on the surface of the water, close to the shore, moving up and down with the swell of the waves. The beginning of freezing? Or what? She's seen the skim of ice forming on the Gatineau and Ottawa rivers. But this would surely be different. How can any water that's so turbulent ever freeze at all? And when the ice does come, it will shut down and smother the waves that she loves so much. Ruefully, she smiles at herself. *Something else to get mad about. I'm really a wreck if I can even get angry at Hudson Bay for freezing.*

By the time Sharla starts to walk home, the sun is low in the sky. Benjamin catches up with her as she moves along La Verendrye Avenue. "We get to have extra hockey practice tomorrow night," he pants, as he runs to keep up with her long legs. "Ever a great rink in the Complex! And your family and friends can watch from that window on the second floor!"

"I know, I know," snaps Sharla. "Do you think I don't know all that? And who's going to watch you, anyway? Not me. That's for sure. And Dad'll be too busy nursing his wounds or watching TV to go. Maybe Mom. She'll come, because she'll be so scared you'll be eaten by bears on the way to and from the rink. As if a hundred-and-twenty-pound woman could save you from a seven-hundred-pound bear, if you happen to meet one at the corner of Selkirk and La Verendrye."

But Sharla can't put even a small dent in Benjamin's pleasure. His round face is shining in the last of the sun.

"She could, too, save me from a polar bear. Besides, we all know what to do if we meet one. Back up slowly. Don't look him in the eye. Or else curl up on the ground with your face down and your arms around your head, and play dead. No big deal." He looks at her eagerly. "Besides," he adds, "I wish we'd hurry up and see one. You know — really close up. *There'd* be a story to tell our grandchildren!"

"If you happened to live to tell the tale," says Sharla. "Anyway, I'm sick of hearing about the stupid bears. Around here, they teach kids the phone number of the Bear Patrol before they even tell them the numbers for the fire department or the Mounties — 555-BEAR."

"Aw, Sharla," complains Benjamin, all the starch gone out of him, "why do you have to be so crabby all the time? It's bad enough having a gloomy father without having a gloomy sister, too. And Mom isn't exactly flying a kite these days." He kicks a tin can someone has left in the center of the road. "I'd kind of like to be happy."

Sharla looks down at him and sees that his brows are squeezed together and that the spark has disappeared from his eyes. She gives him a friendly little punch. "Maybe things'll be better tonight," she says. But she doesn't believe it, not for one minute.

⁕

No one is home when they get there. Sharla lets them in with her key, and then looks around the kitchen, cheerless in the dim afternoon light. She dumps her books in the back porch and then digs two cookies out of the cookie jar for them. Benjamin gobbles his down, without taking off his outer clothes, and then heads for the door.

"I'm gonna play street hockey with Steven and the guys," he says. "We'll be over on Radisson Avenue."

"Keep your mitts on," she says, "or your fingers will freeze and fall off. You can't be much of a hockey player with no fingers."

"Very funny," he says, and slams the door behind him.

Sharla knows she should settle down and

do her homework, but the very thought of all those math problems depresses her. She stretches out on the sofa and stares at the ceiling. *Ottawa. So beautiful in the springtime with all those tulips. Such fun skating on the canal in the winter.* And hanging around the mall with Janice, her best friend, hoping to catch a glimpse of Rick Harrigan from the school football team. Sometimes the whole team would turn up after practice, strutting up and down and hunching their huge shoulders, thinking they were so important. She and Janice would giggle at them behind their hands, but when Rick would pass by, they'd have to hold on to one another to keep from falling over. He was that handsome. Also, eighteen years old and in grade twelve, with a university football scholarship already in his pocket. Sharla smiles at the ceiling, and then sighs. She wonders what Janice is doing these days, and who she's chosen for her new best friend. And how many hearts Rick is breaking, now that he's in college.

And her father. Sharla thinks up words to

describe what he used to be like: busy, warm, *fun*. Kind of nervous, even back then, with a quick temper. But mostly a nice and loving guy. And now the good parts of him seem to be buried deep under the permafrost. Permafrost — a pretty accurate term to describe her father, these days.

Well, maybe she'll watch TV for a while, and then the prospect of homework may start to look more palatable. She curls up on her father's big chair and punches a button on the remote. She's still there when her mother returns at five-thirty. Sharla looks up, already braced to greet that tense face, so full of anxiety and sadness.

Mrs. Dunfield looks different. A little lit up, not quite so strung out.

"Sharla," she announces, "I have a job!"

"Hey, Mom!" Sharla jumps off the couch and turns off the TV. "What? Where? Who hired you? When do you start?"

Her mother laughs. It's a good sound. "Not so fast," she says. "It's no big deal. And it's only temporary — very temporary. But it's *something*. It'll give us a little bit of extra cash during this settling-in period. Until the Ottawa house is sold. Until we can get that big moving bill paid off."

"But *what*? What's the job?"

"Well . . ." Her mother hesitates. "It's at the Tundra Inn, cleaning. You know, changing the beds, vacuuming, doing the bathrooms. It's a busy time of year, and they need extra help. All those bear-watchers coming from all over the world. Every train or plane seems to bring in a whole new batch of them. The hotels are bulging with them. And lots of them are rich. I'm told that they often pay big tips."

Sharla feels worse than ever. Her mother had worked in the accounting department of a big engineering firm in Ottawa. She was a real genius with numbers and computers and every kind of math. *Something that she obviously hasn't passed along to her daughter.* Now she'll be cleaning people's bathrooms.

"And when the bear season's over?" Sharla asks. "What then?"

"I'll probably be laid off, unless part-time work turns up. But they said that if I'm a good worker, they'll take me on again after the winter's over, when the bird season starts. And when the beluga whales come."

Polar bears. Birds. Whales by the thousands, filling up the mouth of the Churchill River. As many as 3,000, in fact. It seems outrageous that this dismal place is apparently so full of wonders. And of course more tourists to clutter up the streets, their humungous cameras dangling from their necks, looking like they own the place.

"Damned tourists," mutters Sharla.

"What?"

"You heard me," snaps Sharla. "Damned tourists, damned bears, damned birds, and damned beluga whales."

Mrs. Dunfield sits down. Her face looks drawn and pinched again. "I thought you'd be pleased," she says. Then, "Where's Benjamin?"

"He's out playing hockey on Radisson."

"It's dark, Sharla. You know you're supposed to keep an eye on things when I'm not home. It's not like you're a little child. But Benjamin's only nine. It's not safe for him to be out at this time of day. Not at this time of year. The bears —"

"Oh, the *bears*!" Sharla is already grabbing her boots and hauling them on. Then her parka and scarf. But no mitts or gloves.

"Sharla! Put your mitts on!"

"Mom!" Now Sharla is yelling. "Get off my back! Quit nagging me! I've got pockets! I don't need mitts!" And she's out the door and gone.

Radisson Avenue is a long street. By the time Sharla finds Benjamin, her hands are beginning to feel sore and numb. "Hurry, you dummy!" she shouts at Benjamin. "You know you're supposed to get home before dark. *Hurry!*"

They run most of the way home, with Sharla wiggling her fingers around in her pockets to keep the circulation going. As they come up the steps to their front porch, they hear angry voices inside. Opening the door, they can see their father's flushed face. Their mother has on her frozen look, and her eyes are swimming with tears.

"No wife of mine," he's yelling, "is going

to spend her days cleaning out other people's toilets! And that's final!"

Benjamin and Sharla slip by them and take off their outer clothes in their rooms upstairs. Sharla shuts her door and sits down on her bed, hugging her hands against her ribs, rocking back and forth. The pain is awful, but she'd die before she'd tell anyone about the chilblains in those fingers.

CHAPTER FOUR

The next day, no one mentions Mrs. Dunfield's job at breakfast time, but after Sharla's father leaves for work, her mother busies herself getting ready to go out.

"You're going to work," Sharla says. It's both a question and a statement.

"Yes."

"But Dad said . . ."

"Yes, I know. But I'm going, and he knows it. He's mad, but he can see that you can't accept a job, sign papers that say so, and then not turn up the next day. So I'm going. Besides . . ."

"Besides?"

"It may give me something to do with my adrenalin. All that good hard physical work."

"Why don't you just let fly with your adrenalin? Why don't you get mad right back when he blasts you?"

"You make it sound so simple, Sharla. But it isn't. We're not little kids in a playground, trying to get even with each other. We're two grown-up people, and one of us is in pretty bad shape. I'm afraid that if I start yelling at your father instead of talking to him, he might fall right apart at the seams. He's like a cracked egg right now, with a very thin shell."

"Well — it's not fair."

"Lots of things aren't fair in this life." Mrs. Dunfield speaks sharply. "So get used to it."

"Oh, thanks, Mom. Thanks a lot. Thanks for your wonderful guidance." Sharla slams her way out the door and trudges up the street to La Verendrye, without looking back.

Well, at least the wind isn't blowing so hard today. It's more like a breeze than a raging gale. And the sun is actually shining. Down on Kelsey Boulevard, she can see a small army of tourists standing around, waiting for yet another expensive bus trip to start. As she passes the Eskimo Museum, Sharla notices a now-familiar figure on the road ahead. The red toque. The short leather jacket. Camera equipment by the gross. He's just standing there.

"Hi," he says, as she comes closer. "I was waiting for you."

"You were what?"

"Waiting for you. I need your help, if you'd consider giving it."

She looks at him carefully for the first time. He's fairly tall, and under his jacket she thinks she sees broad shoulders. Or maybe he has shoulder pads, but she hopes not. He doesn't look all that old. He isn't really *young*, but he doesn't look worn down by life, the way her parents do. His face, under that red toque, is pleasant. In fact, *very* pleasant. He has a straight nose, a broad grin, and kind eyes. *Kind eyes.* She manages a smile.

"What on earth kind of help do you need? Protection from the bears? A new pair of mitts?"

"Cheeky!" he says, and laughs. "But that's OK. I like a woman with spirit. I saw you inside the Complex window yesterday. In fact, I've seen you there a couple of times. And other places. I need two things — someone to hand me lenses and take notes while I'm shooting — for about an hour each day. And also someone to be in some of the pictures, so there'll be a sort of steady presence in my photo essay. It would save me time *and* money if I could find a person who could perform both those functions. And I think maybe you could. I know for sure you've got the kind of look I need for the pictures. I can recognize a face that photographs well. You've got the bones for it. Also, a range of expressions. I've been watching you." Then he adds, "My name is Jake."

Sharla stares at him. Could he be talking about *her*? "What's a photo essay?" *Bones for it?*

"I have an assignment from a magazine in

the States to do an article on Churchill. It's a pretty famous place, you know. I'm an American. This is my first trip north, and I've only been here three days. But if I strike oil on this job, I'll be coming back again in the bird and whale seasons. This is a big article — a long one — and I'll make a bundle if they like it. It'll be mostly pictures, but there'll be some text."

"Wow!" Sharla can't think of another thing to say.

"Yeah, but I also need someone to show me around a bit. Point out some of the things I should include in my essay, so I don't have to waste my time searching them out."

"How would all this save you money?" Sharla finds that she's able to speak again.

"Because if you could be my guide, research assistant, model and gopher for one hour a day, I'd only be paying one person. I said I needed you for two things. I guess I'm not very good at math. That list adds up to four." He grins his amazing grin.

"You're talking about hiring *me*?" Sharla's glad the wind isn't blowing too hard, because if it were, she'd probably fall right over.

"Right. You've got it. I can't pay you much, but I can pay you *something*. Five dollars an hour. An hour a day and two hours a day on weekends. Sometimes maybe more. I've already done the bus tour and the Tundra Buggy thing, so the rest of my essay will be centered around the town. I'll only be here six more days, so I need to pack in a lot of work."

Six more days. Two of them on the weekend. Forty dollars. Maybe I'm not such a dummy at math after all. It's amazing how fast you can multiply if your whole financial life is at stake.

"Well — can you do it?"

"I have some basketball practices, and I'll also have to ask my mom and dad."

Or maybe I don't have to ask them. Sharla doesn't always go home right after school, and maybe some of this can be done at noon, when her parents are working. Besides, they might say No. She stands there, frowning.

"But I need you to start today," he says. "There's not much time. C'mon. *Do it.*"

Sharla only hesitates for a moment.

"You're on," she says.

Jake takes off his toque and scratches his ear. With his head bare, Sharla can see that it's full of crazy black curls. She is loving how great he looks. "Let's see . . ." He's talking again, but Sharla is having difficulty keeping her mind on his words. She's too busy looking. "I know classes knock off around noon, because I've seen the kids pile out of school then. Meet me in front of the library door. We'll hop in my truck and go downtown. That'll save precious time."

"Truck?"

"Yes. I rented Vernon Joudrey's truck for a week. Makes things happen faster for me."

Sharla hears her mother's voice saying, "Never get in a vehicle with a strange man."

"OK," she says. "Ten to twelve."

"Bring a comb," he says.

✢✢✢

The morning crawls by like a turtle, but it also seems quick, because Sharla's thoughts are whizzing around at such a dizzy rate. How can time be both slow and fast at the same time? She shakes her head, and Miss Hendrickson notices, for the hundredth time, that Sharla isn't listening to a word she's saying.

I have a job! With an older man, who must be at least twenty-eight. But with a real neat face and kind eyes. Even better looking than Mr. Kent. *Jake.* An American, working for a big-wheel magazine. *Assisted by Sharla Dunfield, research assistant, guide, model and gopher.* She knows what a gopher is. A gopher goes for things.

Sharla's math problems are a disaster, but how could she be expected to do any good work last night, with that battle raging on the floor below her room?

During the next period, Mrs. Joyce raves on about Shelley; and Mr. Lovitt fights the Siege of Louisbourg during third period. Sharla survives it all, and suddenly it's ten to twelve. She puts her coat and boots on quickly, and dashes to the door, head bare. She doesn't want to be seen getting into that truck.

Jake is parked exactly where he said he

would be, and they take off as soon as she gets in the truck. Once downtown, he parks the vehicle by the Tundra Buggy office, and they walk back towards the central part of town. She shows him the main restaurants, and points out stores where crafts are sold. "You should see the tourists coming out of there," she says, pointing to the Arctic Trading Company, "loaded down with fur mitts and suede coats and parkas and jewelry and books and soapstone carvings. Once I even saw someone haul a five-hundred-dollar bill out of his pocket and toss it on the counter as if it was a Loony."

"A Loony?"

"Yes. Our one dollar coin."

"Why Loony?"

"Because it's got a loon on it. One of our special birds. It's got this really wild, lunatic cry. Haven't you ever heard anyone say 'as crazy as a loon'? Well, that's what they're talking about."

He tells her they have loons in the States, too, but that there aren't many in New York City, which is where he lives.

She shows him the hotels in town, and points out the old railway station, and also what seem like miles and miles of railway cars strung out on the track leading to the grain elevator. She tells him there's no road into Churchill — just planes and trains. She takes him into the Northern Images craft store, and they look at the Inuit dolls, the native jewelry, the bead work.

"There's a soapstone ptarmigan in here I'd die for," she says to Jake, and shows it to him. "Ptarmigans are such great birds — fat and flappy, making their big holes in the snow, and turning white in winter. I love them." She strokes the piece of sculpture, realizing with a start that she hasn't said — out loud — that she loves anything, in a very long time. Well, she loves the waves on the beach when the wind is up, but she thinks that this may all be part of her anger thing. And she sort of loves Mr. Kent, the basketball coach, but he's probably more of a hero than a real live love object. Her feeling for him is all wrapped up in basketball, which she is really and truly in love with. Right now, basketball is the one bright light in her dark night. She figures it wouldn't be all that hard to love Jake — with his curly hair and big grin and *kind eyes* — if only he wasn't so old. But then again, he's probably only about thirteen years older than she is. She'll give that some thought when she goes to bed tonight. Men often marry women who are thirteen years younger than they are.

Every so often Jake takes a picture of Sharla — looking up at the Trading Company sign; in the foreground of the huge grain elevator; bending down to admire the soapstone ptarmigan; and later on, entering the Complex. For most of the pictures he asks her to take off her hood and let her long hair fly in the wind. Once he tells her to comb it. She carries his box of photographic gear, and hands him his lenses or filters or mysterious little squares of grey cardboard, when he asks for them.

When Jake drops her at the school at 1:00 p.m., he hands her a five dollar bill. He grins at her. "You're great," he says. "You're worth much more, but right now, it's all I can pay.

I'm really broke. I'm not one of those rich tourists you seem to hate so much. I'm up here earning my living. My accommodation at the Tundra Inn is paid for by the magazine I'm doing the work for, but I'm a freelancer who's never sure where his next buck is coming from."

The Tundra Inn. Sharla's mother might be changing his sheets and vacuuming his floors and cleaning his bathroom at this very minute. Sharla finds it hard to center her mind on this thought. Does she like that idea or not? No, she doesn't think she does.

All through phys. ed., she keeps thinking about it. What if he hears her mother speaking about her? *Oh, yes, I have a son and a daughter. The daughter's a gangly fifteen-year-old — Sharla's her name — as moody as all get out, and loses her temper at the drop of a hat.* What if Jake writes her name on something — a cigarette box or a scratch pad or whatever — and leaves it lying around in his room? Sharla feels fear clutch her chest with a real physical wrench. What if? What if? If she'd asked her mother's permission to do this job for Jake, all those things would seem a lot simpler. But now it's too late. She's *done* it, and if she asks her now, her mother will know she was sneaky about it in the first place. Sharla doesn't dare to even think what her father would say. Tomorrow she'll tell Jake to park down on Franklin Street. Better not run the risk of having half the world see her getting in and out of that truck every day.

Basketball practice that afternoon is great. She makes four hook shots, and moves around like lightning. She feels as though she's flying. She knows she's good, and so does Mr. Kent. "Looks like you'll make the senior team, Sharla," he says, as she heads for the dressing room. "You're young for it, but if you work hard, I think you can do it. Keep up the good work. *And don't miss any practices.*"

Perfect Mr. Kent, with all that neat red hair. If Miss Hendrickson would just stop scolding her for not getting her homework done, and if Mr. Lovitt wasn't so boring about history, and if Mrs. Joyce wasn't so crazed with love for those dopey poets, she could maybe feel less miserable in this school. Home is a disaster, but Collette's a good friend, and faithful old Theo would be her willing slave if she so much as snapped her fingers. *But now I have my job with Jake, and I can just thumb my nose at Hendrickson and Lovitt and Joyce for five more days. At the end of that time, I'll be rich and probably in love.*

Collette catches up with her on her way home. "Where you been?" she says. "You shot out of school so fast at noon that I figured there must be a crisis somewhere. You OK?"

"Very OK." Sharla tells her about Jake — all of it: the meeting on La Verendrye Avenue, the job proposal, the noontime guided tour, the five dollar bill.

"Does your mom know?"

"Well, no, as a matter of fact."

Collette slaps her forehead with the flat of her hand. "I thought you were dumb about Theo," she says. "But this isn't dumb. This is the act of a maniac. Your parents'll kill you. A strange man — *an older man* — a truck, pictures, money! Maybe they'd think it was fine. Maybe it is. But then again, maybe it isn't. If you start fooling around with a man who's twice your age, who's giving you money and telling you to comb your hair, people are going to have lots of things to say about it behind your back."

Sharla can feel her lips twitching and her breath coming fast. *I wasn't doing anything wrong. Neither was Jake.* Good, kind Jake, with his friendly eyes. Doesn't Collette understand how much she needs someone in her life who has kind eyes? And Collette's eyes are looking so fierce right now. Sharla feels like slapping her until those eyes pop right out of her head. Instead, she takes her own textbooks out of her backpack, one by one, and throws them into a snowbank. Then she runs home as fast as she can make her legs move, unlocks the door, and slams it behind her.

CHAPTER FIVE

At 8:30, the phone rings. By that time, Sharla has spent almost three whole hours in a state of bottled-up anger. But not always bottled-up. Sometimes letting it fly. The *minute* her father came in the door, he'd given her a big lecture on getting to school on time and keeping her grades high, so that she could make it into university in order "to better yourself."

Could you maybe start this conversation by saying, "Hello, Sharla, and how are you this evening, my dear?" And just how did your own years in university serve to improve either your

self or your life? These days she knows
about kids who've done the whole four-year
university stretch, and are selling pencils
door-to-door, or else collecting welfare
checks. Well, she managed to keep all that to
herself. *No point in throwing fire on a bomb
that's already exploded.*

Then, after supper, her mother got on her
back about how her sweater was far too
tight, and didn't Sharla realize that there
were some things she should leave to other
people's imaginations? Sharla had slammed
a mug of milk down on the table, spilling it
all over a clean tablecloth, and yelled, "I
don't tell *you* what to wear. Maybe you'd
like to know how totally uncool I think some
of *your* clothes are. Besides, what's so wrong
with *breasts?*"

"Nothing," said her mother. "But you
don't have to *flaunt* them. That sweater
makes you look like a photograph from
some sleazy girly magazine."

Sharla said nothing. *Bottled-up.* But maybe
not bottled-up. Possibly scared to death.
Had she taken her coat off in the Northern

50

Images store when Jake took that picture of her with the carved ptarmigan? He'd told her to take off her hood and mitts. But no. She remembered. He'd wanted her to look like a tourist contemplating a purchase, so she'd left her coat on. Sharla sighed with relief. But only for a moment. *What kind of magazine will be buying Jake's pictures? Why is he taking so many pictures of me?* Quickly she said to her mother, "Tomorrow I'll wear that tunic I got during my last week in Ottawa, over my leggings. It's loose. I bet you'll be happy to know that *loose* is the *in thing*. If I had two nickels to rub together, I'd buy another tunic from the Sears catalogue. But extreme poverty seems also to be in style this year, so I sure hope my one tunic is washable."

There. She might have known it. She'd spoiled her pleasant little speech with a crappy little dig in the last sentence. That sent her father into the living room to brood, muttering, "Sorry! Sorry! Sorry!" while her mother did a lot of unnecessary clattering around with the dishes in the kitchen.

Finally, her mother sat down. She took Sharla's hand, but Sharla shook it off. "Listen, Sharla," she said. "Being poor isn't the worst thing in the entire world. A huge percentage of the population of our planet is poor to a degree that you can't even begin to understand."

Sharla felt her eyes glaze over. *The Pollyanna Speech. The Count-Your-Blessings Sermon.*

Her mother was still talking. "For one thing, you're not hungry. You've got clothes to wear — be they tight or loose . . ." (she gave a nervous little laugh) ". . . and you have a roof over your head and a room of your own. Some people would kill for that. In fact, some people *do* kill for that. Another thing — there's no one shooting you down when you go outside of your own house. The nearest war is thousands of miles away."

Sharla knew there were things in the Pollyanna Speech that made a lot of sense. But during these last few months, whenever her mother started in on it, Sharla would just switch herself right off. It was all so boring. Mrs. Dunfield could deliver the whole sermon without Sharla hearing one single word.

However, when the speech was over, something made her ask her mother, "How was your job?"

"Fine!" she answered, with what might have been exaggerated enthusiasm. But maybe not. "I like it. I'm out of the house and meeting people. I don't mind physical work, and I'll probably lose a pound or two. The hotel people are nice, and I enjoy meeting the tourists."

"Oh!" sneered Sharla. "The *tourists*!"

"You don't need to sound so scornful and superior, Sharla, just because you think they have a whole lot of money. After all, we once had plenty of money ourselves. And not all of those tourists are rich. Some of them are writers, planning to sell a book or an article about Churchill. Lots of them are photographers with amazing cameras the size of umbrella racks. I find them interesting. I like hearing about the places they come from —

San Francisco, Tokyo, Frankfurt, Stockholm. It's true that some of them are just doing it for fun, but others are making videos or doing photo essays, which they hope they'll be able to sell, later on."

Photo essays. Why did her mother say that? Had she been talking to Jake? Maybe it wasn't too late to ask her if it was OK to work for him? Or maybe much, much too late.

But it's 8:30, and the phone is ringing.

It's Collette. "Go look in your back porch. Your books are in a plastic bag beside the woodpile. I dried them off a little, but you'd better get them outta there and spread them around someplace where it's halfway warm. I couldn't get them *really* dry."

"Thanks, Collette." Sharla feels hot with gratitude, but she's too embarassed to say anything else. Well, she guesses that's better than nothing, but not much. Right now, the person Sharla is most angry at is herself.

In the meantime, Benjamin is in his room, doing his homework. Or so he says. Maybe he just wants to put a floor between himself and all those fireworks. He's a good kid. Sharla knocks on his door and peeks in.

"You OK?" she asks.

"Yep, I guess so," he says, but his face is sad, as he sits at his desk, his book open but upside down.

"I guess *not*," says Sharla, coming in and sitting on the bed. "Spill it, kid."

"We had a hockey practice tonight, and I didn't go. Mom would never let me go by myself in the dark, and she was flaked out on the sofa like she was dying when I got home from school. I guess her new job's pretty hard."

"Did she say that?"

"She didn't have to. I'm not blind. She looked three-quarters dead."

"So you didn't ask her to go with you?"

"No."

"What about Dad?"

"You kidding? Dad's feeling too sorry for Dad to care about something like hockey."

"Maybe not. He might like to get out there and do something nice for someone — like you, for instance. And he might meet some new friends over there. He can be a pretty friendly guy, you know, when his nervous system isn't tied up in knots. Next time, give it a try." Sharla grins at herself. *Is this little pep-talk for Benjamin or for Dad or for me?*

"And you. You weren't home."

"Sorry. Anyway, I'd have had to do my homework."

"Is it done?"

"It isn't even started."

"It's nine-fifteen, Sharla. Better get going on it before a brand new war breaks out down there."

Sharla looks around his room, at the airplanes strung from the ceiling, at the piles of comics on the floor, at the beat-up looking bear that he's loved ever since he was two. Tears sting her eyes. *He's just a little kid. He's too young to be thinking about all this garbage.*

❖❖

Sharla goes down and rescues her books from the back porch. Her parents are on the sofa in front of the blaring TV, holding hands. Both of them are sound asleep.

It's true that her books are still pretty damp. She props them up over the hot air register, and spreads the pages. Then she starts her homework. It's midnight before she finishes. She knows she should have started with her math when her brain was more or less alive, but she leaves it to the end. By the time she gets to it, she's so tired that she scarcely recognizes the difference between a plus and a minus sign.

❖

The next morning, Sharla sleeps through the alarm. By the time she races into school, she's ten minutes late. "That's it!" announces Miss Hendrickson, as Sharla slides into her seat. "Be here at eight tomorrow morning, Sharla. The principal will see you at that time. I'll arrange it."

The rest of the morning isn't much better. Mr. Lovitt pontificates about the feudal system in France, and she can't see what it has to do with studying Canadian history, which is what they're supposed to be doing. She says so, and asks him what on earth connection there is between the two. He says, "You'll see! You'll see!" as though he has an ace up his sleeve. Mrs. Joyce makes them write a class essay on the effect of nature on the poetry of Keats and Shelley. Sharla can't think of enough ideas to fill even half a page.

At noon, Sharla goes up and looks out over the Bay. There's definitely a skim of ice on the surface in many places, and slob ice — almost like slush — is beginning to form in the areas close to the rocks and the beaches. She thinks about the seals out there. "It won't be long," she whispers. "Then you'd better really keep your eyes open."

"Talking to yourself, now, huh?" It's Theo, beside her on the bench. Someone must have told him that she likes to come here. She looks at him and thinks how gangly and pleasant he looks. And his eyes are undeniably kind. Now that she figures she's in love with Jake, she feels oddly comfortable with Theo.

"No," she says. "I was actually talking to the seals. Telling them to be careful. Warning them that as soon as the Bay freezes over, the bears will be moving out onto the ice to gobble them up."

He stands up and gazes out the window. "I love this place, too," he says, sweeping his arm around to include the large area near the big windows. "It's great when the Bay's open. But wait'll you see it when it freezes over. It's awesome. White on white, as far as your eye can see. You'll love it."

"Maybe," she says, her eyes still fixed on the beach. "Maybe not. I like all those smashing angry waves. Makes me feel better."

"Better than what?"

"None of your business," she snaps. Does *no one* know when to shut up and leave her alone?

"They're really great over at Outreach Services," he says.

She stands up, eyes blazing. How *dare* he! "I don't *need* your stupid old Outreach Services!" she rages. "I don't need anything except to have people leave me alone and stop telling me what to do. Like you, for

Sharla

instance. What do you know about me that would make you think I need to visit the dumb old Outreach place? *Nothing!* This is the first real conversation we've ever had. The conservation project doesn't count. That was *work*. This is *real*." She feels as though she's going to burst wide open with the fury that's inside her.

"I do know about you. You're angry. I don't have to have ten conversations with you to find *that* out. You're *deep-down* angry. I can smell anger a mile away."

She can't believe this. "Supposing you *do* smell my anger. It's *mine*. It's not *yours*. You have no right to poke your nosy face into it. I could kill you, I'm so mad."

He stretches his long legs out in front of him, his eyes on the sea. "No doubt you could," he says. "I'm only poking into your business, because for some stupid and totally inexplicable reason, I care about you. And also because . . . " And here he stops.

Sharla is sitting down now, her arms clutched stiffly across her chest. She stares out at the water, brows knotted. She's surprised to hear herself say, "Because what?"

He looks at her for a moment, and then returns to his view of the white caps on the Bay. "Because of my own anger. The anger that was, and the anger that still is."

She turns to stare at him. She can see that his normally kind eyes are fierce and cold. She can feel the tension, just by being beside him.

"Angry at what?"

"I'll give you the short version," he says, "because lunch hour's almost over. Mad at an alcoholic father who drinks most of his pay check and also gets violent when he's blind drunk. Mad at a mother who got fed up and left, five years ago, because she said she'd go crazy if she stayed. But she took off with a stinking tourist who didn't want any kids. So she left me behind. To face the old man stark alone."

"You hate the stinking tourists, too, then?"

"No," he says. "I just hate that particular stinking tourist."

"Does your mom write to you?"

"Yes. Often. But I don't answer. I can't seem to get that one figured out."

Sharla frowns. "That's pretty awful. That's even worse than what I've got."

"Well," he sighs, "maybe yes. Maybe no. It all depends on how each of us reacts to the mess we're in." Then he says, "For a while, I was thinking I might pack it in."

There's a little silence. Then, "And?"

"The Outreach counsellor saved me. I know that sounds melodramatic, but that's exactly what he did. He showed me that putting a rope around my neck wasn't the smartest thing to do with my anger. For one thing, it might make my dad feel bad enough to be sorry and even to learn how to stop drinking. But I wouldn't be around to enjoy it. I'd be down in the permafrost. A pretty simple idea, but it hadn't occurred to me. And it took him a good long time to put it across to me."

A lot of this starts to sound like a lecture to Sharla. But it's interesting, and she can't stop asking questions. "What else did they tell you?"

"Well, to begin with, it wasn't *them*. It was *him*. You only work with one person. And he doesn't just *tell you*. *You* tell *him*. And everything's confidential, just between you and him — or her. But he gave me some pretty sharp clues."

"Like?"

"Well, just for starters, not to get mad at the whole goddamn world if what you're mad at is just one person or situation. Like, I think *you're* always mad at *me* because you're mad at something else. Man, did I do a lot of that! I did it all the time. I was even mad at the *dog*. And at anything that looked like a bottle. I'd search out Dad's boxes of liquor and throw the bottles at the rocks, out behind the Eskimo Museum. Then he'd come home and beat me up. I'd go to school so black and blue that finally someone dragged me, kicking and screaming, over to Outreach Services. I mean kicking and screaming *inside my head*. I didn't want to go. Like you, I figured it was my own business. I didn't want some stranger, some *grownup*, poking around in my own private garbage dump."

"But you don't *seem* angry."

"Most of the time, I'm not anymore. Getting rid of even half of your anger is like dropping a two-ton weight off your back. But I'm still really pissed off about some things. How do you forgive a mother who left her ten-year-old kid with an abusive father? That's not exactly easy to forget. In her letters she tries to explain it. She says that before she left, it was her who was getting beaten up all the time. Not me. She says she figured we'd both — Dad and me — be fine, with her gone. Huh!"

"And your dad? Is it easier to forgive him?"

Theo leans his chin on his fist. "Even when you learn about alcoholism being an illness, how do you stop being angry at someone who seems to love a bottle more than his own *son*? And who kicks me around when he's drunk? He's going to AA now, and he's lots better — but not always. At least he's trying. But I still have a lot of work to do on the anger I feel towards him. That's why I study so hard in school. So I can leave.

I love Churchill so much — the Bay, the long stretches of tundra, the way the light catches the little stubby trees when they're laden with snow, the river all churned up with whales in the summer, the birds. But I want a scholarship so I can get out of here five minutes after I graduate."

This isn't sounding like a lecture anymore. Sharla looks at Theo and thinks about what she'd like to say to him. She speaks the words in her mind. *I'd like to be your friend, Theo. I think maybe I'm in love with someone else, but I really want you for my friend.* She can't say any of those things to him — not right now. But she does touch the back of his fingers with the flat of her hand.

"Thank you, Theo," she says.

CHAPTER SIX

That afternoon, Sharla's hour with Jake is even better than yesterday's. They walk around the edge of the town and notice how the tundra impinges on it from north and south, and how the river borders one side and the Bay the other. Although Churchill sits on a peninsula, it seems almost like an island to Sharla, cut off as it is from the rest of the country by water and by an inhospitable landscape. Jake takes pictures of her beside the tiny trees, in front of the shiny granary ponds, leaning against the bronze statue of two polar bears downtown. A couple of times he arranges her hair so that it blows exactly right in the wind. She loves the feel of his hands brushing against her face. She watches him, liking everything she sees. He gives her another five dollars as they approach the truck for the trip back into the center of town. Then he drops her off at the corner of Radisson and Hearne.

That evening, Sharla does her homework right after supper. She's been thinking about what Theo said about a scholarship being his means of escape. He doesn't even really want to leave Churchill; he loves everything about it, even the merciless wind. And it's the place where he once had a mother and was happy. But Sharla guesses he feels he has to get far away from his father if he's going to survive — not survive like living instead of dying; survive like having a real life for himself.

Well, Sharla does want to leave Churchill. She wants to leave *everything*. Collette's a good friend, and Mr. Kent's a great coach, but that isn't enough. In four days, Jake will be gone until he returns in the spring for his bird pictures. *If* he returns. Maybe he'll write. How can she stand it if he doesn't? He must like her, or else why would he have chosen her out of the whole town full of people? He must have stood outside the school and looked at all the kids spilling out of the door, and then chosen *her*. That must mean *something*. But she can't be sure exactly what. Or how much.

And if Theo goes away to college, who'll be left in this place to understand what makes her tick — who'll see her wheels going around, and know what it's all about? No. She might as well study and aim at a scholarship. She needs an exit door, too.

That night, Sharla has many dreams. The first one is a nightmare. She's running, running, running over the frozen tundra. She's in her flannelette nightie, and her feet are bare. It's very cold. She's frightened, but she doesn't know why. She just has to run and run, in order to escape something. She knows she isn't moving fast enough, and that soon the mysterious something is going to catch up to her. Suddenly, she trips on a rock and falls down, down, down into a black hole. She puts both hands over her eyes and screams, but her throat is paralyzed and no sound comes out. When she hits the ground at the bottom of the hole, she wakes up. Her feet are out of the covers, and the room is cold.

For a while, she's afraid to go back to sleep for fear of finding herself right back in the same dream. But in spite of her fears, she falls asleep again, quite soon. In a new dream, she's getting into the truck with Jake. It seems to be spring, because their heads are bare and she feels such a warm sense of hope and lightness. Jake's black curls are glistening in the sun, and his face is full of his love for her. They are parked near the door leading into the library, and all the kids are standing around, watching. Suddenly, they start to clap. They keep clapping and clapping, and the sound makes her very happy. But far down the road at the edge of the Complex building, she can see Theo. He's just standing there, with his back turned, facing nothing except the end of the town and the barren ground. When Sharla wakes up, she feels both peaceful and troubled. It takes her a long while to go back to sleep.

When the alarm goes off, Sharla wakens with a start: 7:15. She has three-quarters of an hour to get dressed, have her breakfast, and get to school by eight. Better skip breakfast. No time. This is one day when she'd better not be late.

Sharla sits outside Mr. Shard's office and waits. The waiting is awful. She doesn't really know the principal, but she's heard that he doesn't put up with what Collette calls "any foolishness." She heard one girl say that compared to Mr. Shard (shard — a dagger of glass), Miss Hendrickson is just a pussycat.

Finally, the door opens. "Come in, Sharla," he says. He doesn't ask her to sit down, and he wastes no time in getting down to business.

"It's only October 28th, Sharla," he says, "and I see by this attendance record that you've been late for school six times. We've been easy on you because you're new, and we realize that sometimes it's hard to adjust to a new school. But to be late six times is inexcusable. It's disturbing to the class and to the teacher, and also means that you're apt to miss the start of the lesson. This other record . . ." (he points to another set of papers in the folder) ". . . indicates that your grades aren't up to snuff. You're barely passing math, and Mr. Lovitt says that your attitude in class is very negative. You've been tested, and we therefore know that your IQ is unusually high. So there has to be a reason why you only seem to be excelling in phys. ed. and basketball."

He pauses and looks at her, pursing his lips. "Mr. Kent," he continues, "tells me that if you keep up the good work, you should make the Senior Basketball Team. Congratulations. However, basketball alone can't take you very far in this life. If you want to go to university, you'll have to do something more productive than run around a gym. You've got to get those grades up, and fast. So . . . " He pauses again. And then goes on:

"So I've reluctantly come to a decision. For the next three weeks, I'm not permitting you to go to basketball practice. Instead, I'm asking you to use that time for extra math and history. Your English assignments have been poor, too, so you'll be working on English as well. And if you choose to be late for school even once during that three weeks, I'll ask Mr. Kent to keep you out of that gym until the Christmas break."

Sharla doesn't move, but her breath is coming very fast. She hopes she can get out of the office before she does something awful, like throw that chair at the wall, or (worse still) break into screaming tears. Her throat is so tight that she knows she'd be unable to speak.

"That'll be all, Sharla. I'd like you to report back to me at the end of the first week, I've asked the teachers to do the same thing. In the meantime, you might consider getting some counselling over at the Health Centre." He doesn't look at her as he says this.

Sharla turns around and leaves the room.

She also leaves the building. Then, remembering Mr. Shard's final words about being late, she immediately turns around and re-enters the school. She goes directly to her classroom, and sits down at her desk. She refuses to let herself cry, but she thinks she may burst from her effort to hold back the tears. Like a stone statue she sits there, waiting for class to begin, hands clasped together on the desk, knuckles white, eyes straight ahead. Collette stops at her desk and asks, "You OK, Sharla? You look awful." But Sharla can't answer. When Theo sees her, he comes over and stands beside her.

"What happened?"

But all she can do is shake her head.

Something in Sharla's appearance must be warning the teachers away that morning, because no one asks her a single question or demands anything of her. When the lunch-bell rings, she puts on her outside clothes and rushes out of the school. Running along the side of the building facing La Verendrye Avenue, she reaches the road that leads down to the beach. She *needs* that beach. The crashing waves are the only language she'll be able to understand today. Passing the Bear Alert sign, she finally comes to a halt on the edge of the beach. The tide is low, and the area is encrusted with frozen seaweed and chunks of ice. But the water is still open, and the wind is strong. The waves are pounding down on the sand and gravel, one after the other, with almost no backwash between them. She feels as though she *is* the sea.

And then, far over to the right, way beyond the southern edge of the Complex, she senses movement of another kind. Sharla's vision is good, but she squints in order to make it better. What has she seen — or almost seen — among those dark rocks over there? When the movement catches her eye again, she knows what she is seeing. She stares, frozen with fascination, as the bear's head appears above one of the rocks. Then, as she holds her breath, he stands on his hind legs and rises to his full height. He must be nine or ten feet tall. He's looking at her, and he's stretching up for a better view.

We're watching one another. He's a long way off, so she feels she's in no immediate danger. Still, she backs up slowly, avoids looking directly into the bear's eyes, and wills him not to move. Then, turning around, she races as fast as her legs can take her across the back of the beach and up towards the road leading to La Verendrye Avenue.

As Sharla turns the corner, she can see a white shape moving swiftly towards her from the rocks where she first glimpsed the bear. In her head, she hears the description of a polar bear's speed: *Faster than any human being can run.*

Rushing into the library, she pants the words out to Mrs. Cole: "A bear! Coming along the road behind the Complex! Please! Call the Bear Patrol for me!" Then, yelling, "Bear! Bear!" she tears up to the upper foyer and watches from the window.

There he is, walking now, slowly, sedately, with the smooth grace of a dancer, moving along the beach. She can see how huge he is, how beautiful. She feels a strange constriction in her chest that has nothing to do with fear. It has to do with awe, with wonder. Briefly, she remembers Collette's words: "You'll fall in love, just like the rest of us."

A crowd has formed around her, and they all watch as the Bear Patrol van comes into view. An officer emerges, holding his cracker shell gun and firing upwards. Light and sound explode into the air, and the bear stops for a moment as though uncertain of his next move. Then he turns and races off towards the south, not stopping until he is out of sight.

After everyone else has left, Sharla stands alone at the window. Her lips are moving, but her words are silent.

I've seen a polar bear. Everything else in my life is wrong right now, except for that one amazing fact. Without paying out a fortune of money, I just turned my head and there, right in front of my eyes, was my bear. Standing on his hind legs. So enormous, so dignified, so elegant. Looking at me. Me, Sharla Dunfield.

Sharla is something of a heroine that afternoon. She was the one to see the bear. It was she who rushed in to sound the alert. No need to tell anyone where she was when she first saw him. She can't handle any more flack today. She'll tell Jake when she sees him after school.

CHAPTER SEVEN

When she tells Jake about the bear, several
different emotions are visible on his face.
Fear is one. "What were you doing down
there, you crazy kid?"

She doesn't let that one pass. "I've seen
you on the beach myself," she says. "From
the Complex window."

"That's different." This time he looks
angry.

Now *she* is angry. "It's not one bit different," she snaps. "You may be a man, but
you wouldn't last two minutes if you had to
take on a bear. I saw him. He was huge. And

powerful. And I bet I can run a whole lot faster than you can."

Fear and anger. Those she has just seen in his face. But now she sees something else. Excitement. His eyes are alive with it.

"I'm going back there in the truck tomorrow," he says. "Behind the Complex. And I'll just wait. Who knows what may happen? I'll bring some food. They say a bear can smell a seal from fifteen miles away, so I'll cart along a big chunk of beef for bait. I took some good pictures from the Tundra Buggy, and the guides were fantastic. But I'd give a whole lot of money to get some photos of a bear with the Bay in the background. With the *open* Bay right behind him. That would make my editors sit up and take notice."

"I don't know about the meat." Sharla frowns. "Baiting a bear sounds pretty dangerous to me."

"I've only got three more days." Jake speaks sharply. "I have to make every one of them count."

They wander around the upper part of the town in the afternoon, and he photographs her in the little prefab Anglican church, shipped over from England and placed on the opposite side of the river in 1892. In 1929, the church was moved again, to the side of the river they're now on. They spend time in the Eskimo Museum, where Jake takes pictures of her beside the enormous stuffed bear and among the Inuit sculptures. They walk under the Baker Lake wall hangings in the Complex, and watch the little kids sliding down the bear slide.

Suddenly, Jake leaves her and climbs the steps into the upper part of the giant bear. Then, with a whoop, he slides down, and pops out the other end, laughing his head off.

"Now you do it," he says, but she won't. She admires him for not worrying about what people think of him, but it matters a lot to her how she looks to others. She needs to be able to keep her cool, and how can she do that if she starts acting like a five-year-old kid?

Most of the students from her school have gone home, but she knows a few of them must still be hanging around the Complex

— at the Launching Pad, at the tables on the upper floor, down in the library. Suddenly she discovers that she doesn't care who sees her with Jake. Her experience with the principal and her adventure with the bear are mixed up in her head in a way that she doesn't even try to figure out. All she knows is that she feels reckless — not reckless enough to go down the slide, but ready to take some chances. Being with Jake isn't doing anything wrong. She isn't even skipping basketball practice, because it doesn't exist for her any more. Things can't get much worse at home, even if her mother finds out about Jake.

"How's the Tundra Inn?" she asks, out of the blue, not looking at him. He's fixing her hair behind her shoulder for a shot of her with a little pre-schooler in the indoor playground.

"It's good. The office staff are helpful with directions and stuff, and the food's great."

"How about the rooms? Do they keep them neat and clean?" *Am I really asking this?*

"Clean as a whistle. A really nice woman

looks after mine. She's cute, too. Little, and quick on her feet. If I wasn't too busy, I might ask her for a date."

Cute. A date. No. It couldn't be.

"What does she look like? Maybe I know her. It's a small town."

"Oh, about five-foot-two, nice figure, smooth short hair that tucks under a little at the bottom. Turned-up nose. A very pretty chick. Always seems to wear blue."

Her mother, all right. *A very pretty chick.* And where did he get that chick stuff?

"Do you figure you know her?" Jake is curious.

Sharla hesitates before she answers. She seems to be swimming in water that's getting deeper and deeper. "I don't know," she says. "Lots of people come and go in this town. They work for a while and then get out."

Why did I ever ask him about the Tundra Inn? Sharla's mind feels like a whirlpool, with a confused jumble of thoughts and events being sucked down into it. The principal made her seem like a criminal, only this morning. Basketball is forbidden territory for three whole weeks. So I'm sad as well as bad. Then the bear episode turned her into a heroine for half the afternoon. On top of all that, Sharla feels hemmed in by all the secrets she's not telling her family. She can't seem to center on anything.

Suddenly she says, "I just want to escape. Let me go with you when you go to the beach tomorrow. You'll need someone to hand you lenses and stuff."

"Well, I dunno," he mutters. "You're a minor, and we'd be sort of breaking the law. Not exactly, but we're sure not supposed to be wandering around down there."

"Please," Sharla begs. "*Please*, Jake."

"Oh, well," he says. "OK. But only if you do something for me."

"Yeah? What?"

"Let me tag along with you on Halloween. I'd like to use my high speed 1600 ASA film to get some night pictures. Halloween's this Saturday. Or is it tomorrow?"

"Sunday. I know, because Mom and Dad are going to be in Thompson on the weekend and won't be back till the plane gets in on Monday. I have to keep an eye on Benjamin when he's trick-or-treating, so that he won't get chewed up by any bears. You can come with us. You can check out the Bear Patrol and the RCMP to see how they protect us, and maybe get some neat shots of the searchlights scanning the shore. Even the fire department comes out to keep the kids safe. Everyone will be carrying food, and that's a no-no if there's any bears around. This is my first Halloween here, too. It should be kind of creepy."

Jake climbs back in his truck. "I'm off to get some pictures of the Polar Bear Jail and the Northern Studies Centre. See you tomorrow. Where do we meet this time?"

"On the road leading down to the beach," she says. "Park there. I'll join you as soon as school's out."

"No basketball?" he asks.

"No," she says. "No basketball."

❖

As she walks home, Sharla's thoughts are

still crisscrossing one another. The bear — scary, but wonderful in a way she can't even begin to describe or understand. Her mother — a pretty chick. Cute. A twenty-eight-year-old man shouldn't be thinking about her mother like that. Sharla tries to conjure up a clear image of her mom in her head. Is she really a cute and pretty woman? Well, maybe so. She feels a strange but certain pleasure at the thought. Her mother is a person, then, not just her mom or her dad's wife. She tries not to think about Mr. Shard and basketball. Mr. Kent will never let her on the team if she has to miss all those practices. She wants to punch Mr. Shard in the stomach, but she's confused by so many things today, that her despair is on hold. In the meantime, she can look forward to tomorrow's adventure on the beach with Jake.

❖

When her mother opens the door, she does not look like a cute and pretty chick. She looks like a tired and furious mother.

"Who is he?" She speaks before Sharla

can even get inside the house. Her voice is louder than it usually is. Sharla's heart begins to ricochet around inside her chest. She knows what's coming.

"Who's who?" She's stalling for time.

"You know precisely what I'm talking about, Sharla Dunfield," says her mother. "People have been telling me things. They aren't tattling. They just mention all this as though it's old news to me. I've had to pretend I knew."

"Knew what?"

"About the tourist you're wandering all over town with. In his truck. Walking. In the stores. In the Complex. Apparently everywhere."

"I'm not doing anything wrong, Mom."

"Then may I ask why you haven't told me anything about him? You're only fifteen years old, and I happen to be your mother. Your father's going to have a fit." Mrs. Dunfield stops talking for a moment and rubs her fingers back and forth across her forehead. "What are you doing with him? Mrs. Charles says she saw him combing your hair. And I found five dollars in your jeans pocket when I did a wash this afternoon."

Sharla's chest feels like a lead weight. She wills herself to be calm, and not to go stomping out of the room. "He's OK, Mom. I'm working for him. He's doing a photo essay about Churchill, and needs someone to pass him his lenses and even sometimes to pose in front of something — like the train station or the bear statue down on Hudson Square. Sometimes he has to fix my hair so that the picture will be exactly right. Mom — he doesn't do anything wrong. Neither do I. He's a wonderful guy. He pays me five dollars an hour." Then she adds, "I really need some money of my own, and I was afraid you'd say No."

Mrs. Dunfield sits down on a kitchen chair and lets out a long sigh. "I feel as though my whole life is out of control," she says. "The move. Dad's job. The way he's changed. You and your secrets. Who is this man, Sharla?"

Sharla is biting her thumbnail. "He's a

photographer, Mom. I guess I have to tell you that he's staying at the Tundra Inn. His name is Jake something. I forget his last name. I don't think he even told me what it is. You've probably seen him around the hotel. He's got black curly hair, and he's nice. Stop worrying. It's almost the first fun time I've had since I got here." She starts to cry. She's crying about Jake and how she feels about him, and about the bear and the principal and the basketball team, and also about the fact that she has about a million hours of homework to do if she's ever going to get caught up.

Her mother comes over and puts her arm around her. "When you get to be my age," she says, "and have a fifteen-year-old daughter, all this will make sense to you. It does make sense to me. I was fifteen once, and I remember the kinds of things I wanted to do and even some of the ones I did do. And they weren't always what my mother wanted for me. But I'm old enough now to know that things aren't always what they seem. Sometimes danger lurks around the corner in unexpected places. Sharla, I'm sorry, but I'm asking you to stop seeing that man."

Sharla knows about some of those dangers. She's seen some of her friends get into a mess of trouble, even in civilized old Ottawa. She also knows with certainty that she intends to flirt with a polar bear tomorrow, and that she'll be doing it with Jake. She wonders what her mother would feel if she knew *that*. Or that the principal had lowered the boom and banned her from basketball practices for three whole weeks. Or that Jake will be joining her for Halloween night.

"Mom," she says. "I've decided to pull up my socks and study more. And get to school on time. I'm going upstairs right now to do my math homework."

Well, thinks Sharla, at least that much is the truth.

CHAPTER EIGHT

That night, Sharla has another dream. She's standing on the rocky shore of the Bay, facing a full-grown polar bear. They're staring at one another, not moving. She's feeling a mixture of fascination and terror. She knows that she's trapped and that there's no escape for her. Suddenly someone picks her up and carries her back into the Complex. She feels an overwhelming sense of peace and safety. The person who is carrying her is, of course, Jake.

Sharla wakes up with a start, and then lies there, savoring sensations of warmth and comfort. But it's 2:30 a.m., and she hears sounds from the first floor. Hurriedly putting on her slippers and a sweater, she goes to the head of the stairs. The light is on in the kitchen, and she hears a small muffled cough. Her mother's down there.

When Sharla enters the kitchen, her mother is sitting at the table. She's staring straight ahead of her, and her hands are wrapped around a steaming cup of hot milk.

"Mom!" says Sharla. "What on earth are you doing down here? Do you know what time it is?"

"Couldn't sleep," says her mother. "They tell me that hot milk will knock you right out. I'm giving it a try." She sends a small, thin smile in Sharla's direction.

"But why? How come you're not sleeping?" But Sharla thinks she knows why. Her mother isn't sitting there thinking of Jake as someone who is carrying her daughter to peace and safety. No. Sharla just bets that she's wondering how she can bear to leave Churchill while Jake is still in town.

"Oh, I don't know, Sharla," says her mother. "I just sort of know that I ought to be in two places at the same time, and I can't be. You often babysit other kids, so why not your own brother? Still . . . "

"Mom! We'll be fine."

"And I've seen Jake around the Tundra Inn. He does look like a pleasant person. At least his room isn't overflowing with liquor bottles." She gives a little laugh. Then, "Besides, I've asked you not to see him again, so the problem's solved. Still . . . "

"Why do you keep saying *still*? You've got nothing to worry about!"

"If I could only let your father go to Thompson alone, but I can't. We're seeing a lawyer and a real estate person, and there may be papers I'll need to sign."

Oh, please don't stay home. Please.

Her mother continues. "They were good enough to arrange to see us on the weekend, because neither of us can take that much time off during the week. Besides . . . "

"Besides what?"

"Your dad has been looking forward to this trip for so long. I can't bear to disappoint him."

"Then don't!" Sharla wonders if she's sounding kind of frantic. Because that's what she is.

Mrs. Dunfield sighs, and says, "I'm probably being old-fashioned about all of this. Perhaps. Perhaps not. But I just wish my life was a little bit simpler right now."

"Mom . . . " Sharla hesitates. "Does Dad know about . . . you know . . . "

"No," says her mother. "He's got enough to worry about at the moment, without that. Besides, that whole business is all over with now."

Sharla tries not to think about what her mother has just said. She'd better make her mind go blank before she starts seeing things she doesn't want to see. She comes close to her mother's chair, and puts her hand on her shoulder.

"Look, Mom," she says, "you've got a nice trip ahead of you. Don't spoil it by being a wreck tomorrow morning. Go on up and get some sleep. I think that hot milk of yours is starting to work already."

"Maybe you're right," says Mrs. Dunfield,

and gives Sharla's hand a little squeeze. "It's been good to be able to talk about all those things. Thanks, Sharla."

Sharla goes back upstairs, her mind still as blank as she can keep it.

❖

Mr. and Mrs. Dunfield leave for Thompson by plane on the following day, and won't be back until Monday. Sharla's been given strict orders to keep an eye on Benjamin when he's at home, and to check in with his friend Steven's mother if they have any problems. There's a whole page of instructions about Halloween night sitting on the kitchen table.

The wind is up again today, and Sharla is glad of it. It suits her mood. But the sun is bright, and when she goes for her daily viewing of the Bay, she likes the way it hits the side of the iced rocks and makes them shine. The sea looks different this morning, it looks muted, and it takes a moment for Sharla to notice the way the slob ice is gathering among the rocks to the left of the beach and out from the shore for maybe fifty feet. Waves are still breaking on the sand, but Jake had better hurry with those pictures if he wants to photograph a bear in front of an open sea. Yesterday she heard someone in the Northern store say, "If it keeps this cold, the Bay could be frozen over by Monday. Or even by Halloween night. And don't think the bears don't know. They'll be around to check it out. They're hungry. They're itching to get out there and sink their teeth into a fat seal or two."

When the Bay fills with ice, it won't be an angry sea any more. It'll be white and silent and frozen like Sharla's mother when her dad gets into one of his rages. *And when the water freezes over, what am I going to do with my own anger?* She looks at the scene in front of her — the icy rocks with the white tide-line, the sea racing before the savage wind, the snow blowing sideways off the frozen tundra — and thinks, I see now why Theo loves it all so much. You know you're alive in a place like this. Something that wild and fierce can't be dead. It's cold and it's hard. But it's real.

❖❖❖

After school, Jake is waiting for her in the truck on the road leading down to the beach. Benjamin is spending the afternoon at Steven's house, so she is free, free, free until at least four-thirty.

"I was actually able to get some seal meat," he says. "We'll put some of it on the beach, and keep some inside the truck in case we need it later for bait. Get those lenses ready, Sharla. If this works, it could mean one big fat contract for me. And I need it. But I've got to get that picture, contract or not. It's the picture that matters to me."

Sharla looks at him. Inside the truck it's warm, so he has his toque off. His jacket is open, showing a white, fisherman's-knit sweater under it. He may not have much money, she thinks, but he sure looks like he does. I know what the right clothes are, and he's got them. Red wool hat. Leather jacket. Classy sweater. And there, up on the dashboard, is a pair of suede fur-lined mittens, obviously new, obviously expensive. "*. . . it's all I can pay. I'm really broke.*" Never mind.

He looks terrific. His profile is spectacular. That rugged, kindly face has so much more character, more appeal, more *sex* appeal, than the faces of most of the boys she knows, even the ones in grade twelve. They're smooth-skinned and rosy-cheeked, or else pimply; and they have an untried, untested look. But not Jake. As he steps out of the truck to place the seal meat on several places at the edge of the beach, she thinks: I could never marry anyone but an older man.

While they wait, she talks. She tells him about her family's move to Churchill and the anger she often feels at everybody and everything: her parents, most of her teachers, the principal, the rich tourists, and until yesterday, even the non-existent bears. Sometimes, the whole town. She's grateful that he's really listening to her, sometimes saying things like "Hmm!" or "Uh-huh!" But all the while, he's scanning the beach to the south, and fingering his camera, checking the f-stop settings. The windows are down a couple of inches, to keep them from steaming up.

Suddenly he interrupts her in a hoarse whisper. "I see movement over there. Over in the rocks. It could be a bird, but then again, it might be something better. Get ready with the lenses. The wind's coming from the north, which is the right direction for a bear to get a whiff of that meat. If he comes after it, we'll only be a few yards from him."

Sharla feels excitement shoot through her chest. To heck with her parents, the town, the principal, the poverty, the basketball team. This is real living, and she's doing it with someone who's perfect — who obviously respects and trusts her. Who listens to her. And isn't afraid to take chances. She glances up at the Complex window. There's a form up there, but she can't make out who or what it is. She hopes Collette is watching. She'll see what it means to live in the fast lane.

"Look!" Jake is pointing. There, coming around the edge of a large rock, is a bear. He's walking with the slow delicate tread that is now familiar to Sharla, with each step retracting the foot to its strange graceful position, each huge paw set down with such care and certainty. She can sense her breath quickening, her heart beating faster. She's frightened, but the heavy truck gives her a sense of security. Safe and unsafe at the same time. The bear is still a long way off, but he's coming closer with each deliberate step, and he's certainly headed in their direction. He stops for a moment, lifting his head as though sniffing the air, and then starts to move forward again, more swiftly.

But as the bear draws closer, it's clear that he isn't heading towards the meat that Jake has placed on the edge of the beach. He's heading for the truck. Why? And suddenly Sharla knows the reason.

"Jake!" she whispers. "He's coming after the meat in the truck. It's hot in here, and that's the scent that's reaching him strongest. Close the windows!"

"No!" he snaps. "The windows'll cloud up with our breath, and it'll be impossible to get a good shot. I didn't spend an hour cleaning those damned windows, just to have them fog up and wreck my pictures."

"But —" Her voice is no longer a whisper.

"Shut up, you little fool! He'll hear us!" Jake's voice is low, but very fierce. "Now, get ready to hand me what I ask for."

The bear is no more than seven yards away, then five, then three. Jake is shooting, shooting, the camera clicking crazily, recording every move the bear is making. Now the animal is shaking his head from side to side, making noises in his throat that are audible through the partially open window.

Then, suddenly, the bear is on his hind legs, his giant paws on the driver's door, pushing, pushing, and then leaning back, in order to slam forward with more force.

"The horn!" shouts Sharla. "Honk the horn! It might scare him away. Bears can break windows! They tell us that in school. *I know what I'm talking about!*"

When Jake doesn't move to touch the horn, she yells, "Are you trying to kill us?"

"Shut up!" He shouts at her this time, and turns to her with such fury that she feels as though he has struck her. Even in the terror

of the moment, she can see that his eyes are not friendly, are not even marginally kind.

Then he returns to his shooting, taking close-ups of the paws, the nose on the window, the open mouth with its terrifying teeth. He grabs the equipment he needs from Sharla's lap, because she's too frightened to hear what he's asking for. The bear continues to slam against the side of the truck body, the door, the window. And all the time, she can hear her own voice, as though it were someone else's, crying, "Please! Please! Please!" over and over again. When a paw appears at the opening of the window, she crouches over in the corner of the truck, covering her face with her hands. *This is it*, she thinks, and sees through her fingers that Jake is squeezing over to the passenger's seat, and is fumbling to reach the horn. She hears the sound of shattering glass, and suddenly the bear's hot breath is in the cab. His paw is reaching, reaching, for the meat on the front dash, under the windshield.

Then there's a muffled crack, and the bear

shudders before he staggers sideways. As Sharla lets herself watch, she sees the bear slide away from the window, and hears the thud of his body as it hits the side of the truck.

Sharla experiences a moment of numb relief, and now she's whispering, "Thank you. Thank you." But almost before she can believe that they're safe, a Bear Patrol van comes up alongside the truck, and one of the officers yells out, "Stay in there! Don't move until we say so!"

From her cramped position in the corner, Sharla can see that the bear is up again and moving — walking slowly, awkwardly, towards the beach. He looks spastic, unco-ordinated. Why is he walking like that? What's happened to his firm, confident gait? She heard what she thought was the cracker shell gun, but could they actually have shot the bear and wounded him?

Jake remains squeezed over on her side of the truck. There's not much glass left in the window now, and he knows the bear is close, and also unpredictable. They sit like that, their fear still alive, for what seems like forever. In fact, it's little more than ten minutes. Then, suddenly, the bear slumps to the ground and lies there without moving. An officer approaches the animal quietly, carefully, and touches him with the end of his gun. There's no movement. Then he presses his side with his foot — at first gently, and then more firmly.

Sharla watches all of this with growing horror, and discovers that she's yelling at Jake, "He's shot! They've killed him, and it's all your fault! Because of your damned pictures. He was beautiful and enormous and alive, and now he's dead, and it didn't have to happen. I hate you! I *hate* you!"

The orange-suited Bear Patrol officer is at the window. "Open up!" he's shouting. Jake crawls back into the driver's seat and opens the door. "I'm sorry," he croaks, his voice barely more than a whisper. "I didn't know."

"Didn't know what?" yells the officer. "Can't you read? Didn't you see the Bear Alert sign? Do you think these animals are teddy bears? Anyone who's gone out with a

Tundra Buggy tour knows what to expect from a bear, and what to watch out for. And you've been out. I've seen you get on the bus outside the hotel."

Then the man looks across at Sharla, who is still squeezed into the corner of the front seat. "And you, Sharla Dunfield, you live here. How could you be so stupid as to bait a bear? We'll be lucky if there aren't five more bears out here by nightfall. This is like two people throwing matches into a pile of dynamite to see if they can make a big bang." He stretches out his hand. "Give me that meat." Then he says to Jake, "There's a fine for this, you know."

As Jake passes him the package of seal meat, the officer keeps muttering, "Stupid! Stupid!" Someone on the edge of the beach is picking up more of the meat and putting it in a plastic bag.

Sharla gets out of the truck slowly and walks over to where the bear is lying. She can't believe his hugeness, the sense of his power, his perfect coat, his lovely face. She bends over, and touches him on his back, burrowing her fingers into his fur, feeling its thickness. She feels so much love for this dead bear, that she can hardly endure it. She puts her hand on the top of his head and then covers her face so that no one can see how hard she's crying. "He's dead," she's sobbing, "and we killed him."

The officer looks at her kindly. "He's not dead," he says. "We tranquilized him. They're coming over right now to take him away and put him in the Compound, the Polar Bear Jail, until the Bay's frozen hard enough to let him go. You're a crazy kid who should know better, but you didn't kill the bear."

Then he looks at Jake and says, "Turn Vernon Joudrey's truck around and take this kid home, so she can cool off and recover from her shock. If you get to the garage fast enough, maybe they can replace the window before they close." He stares hard at Jake, frowning, "I'll pick up your fine tomorrow," he says. "I know where you're staying. Now, get out! Don't let me find you on this beach again!"

As Jake and Sharla drive away, Sharla looks back and sees the vehicle arriving with the stretcher for the bear. He'll be OK. In a month's time, he'll be walking across the ice with his steady careful movement. He'll be stepping over the ice floes with a grace that she couldn't possibly master. She is amazed that she can love with such intensity a creature that could have so easily torn her to pieces.

Before she gets out of the truck, Jake turns to her. "I'm sorry, Sharla. We could be dead. I realize that. And it was my fault. I should have sounded the horn. I should have driven away. It's just like my daughter always says —"

"Your daughter?"

"Yes. She's about your age. She says to me, 'Dad, you like your pictures more than you like people.' She's right. I get kind of wild if I think I'm going to get a winning shot." He laughs. Then, "Are you OK? Will you go through life terrified of bears?"

His daughter. She has to force herself to think before she answers. "Probably," she says, slowly. "But also loving them. Even though I was sure I was going to die, I couldn't stand it when I thought the bear was dead. Work that one out. I can't."

He gets out of the truck and opens the door for her. She looks at him — hard. I'm seeing a different person from the one I saw three hours ago. How could I start loving a bear so fast? And stop loving a man just as quickly?

"Is Halloween still on?" he asks.

She's buried inside her own head, and doesn't hear his question.

"Is Halloween still on?" he asks again.

She sighs. "I guess so," she says. "But your daughter was right. You do care a lot more about pictures than you do about people — or bears, for that matter. Otherwise you wouldn't be thinking about Halloween right now." Suddenly she feels very, very tired.

"What about tomorrow? It's Saturday. We could do a couple of hours in the morning."

She thinks for a moment. "No," she says. "I don't think so. Mom and Dad don't want me working for you, and I think I'm in too much hot water already. Halloween night's different. I have to go out with Benjamin anyway, so there's no reason why you can't come, too. It's a free country."

He doesn't argue with her. "Here," he says, handing her five dollars.

She waves his hand away. "No thanks," she says. "Use it to buy another pair of fur-lined mittens. I know how hard up you are for money."

She walks into the house like a sleep-walker. As she takes off her parka, her mitts, her scarf, she feels a tear rolling down her cheek. Her mind is acting like a derailed train, slipping and sliding in ten different directions. *His daughter.* She certainly isn't going to forget today in a hurry.

CHAPTER NINE

Sharla doesn't sleep well that night. In her waking thoughts and in her dreams, she keeps reliving that moment in the truck when the window finally broke. She tosses back and forth on the wrinkled sheets, trying to find a comfortable position. But her whole system is too hepped up to let her relax, and she feels stiff and weary when she gets out of bed in the morning. The wind, which has roared around the house all night, is still rattling the windows. Although her own window is closed, Sharla can see the blue-checked curtains moving back and forth in the cold room. The windows aren't tight enough to keep out all the wind.

When she enters the kitchen, Benjamin is already preparing to go outside. Sharla goes out and watches him as he picks up his skates in the back porch and checks the laces.

"Special hockey practice at the Complex," he says. "Gotta go. Steven's mom asked me to lunch. I'll be home by suppertime."

"Before dark," she says. "*For sure*. Did you get some breakfast?"

"Yeah, yeah, yeah," says Benjamin, and slams the door behind him.

It's Saturday. No school, no basketball, no job with Jake. She feels depressed and vacant as she shuffles back into the kitchen for some toast and peanut butter.

The phone rings. "It's Collette," says a small voice on the other end of the line. "I need to see you. I need to talk to you."

"C'mon over," says Sharla. The last time she had a real conversation with Collette, she'd been mad enough to want to slap her across the face. But that seems a long, long time ago now. "I'll make some hot chocolate." Better let Collette know that she's still her best friend. After all, she rescued Sharla's books from the snowbank, and even tried to comfort her after her interview with the principal. And right now, Sharla can't even remember why she'd been so mad at her. Something about her and Jake. Yes.

Collette lives three blocks away, but she's knocking at the Dunfield's door within five minutes. When she comes into the kitchen, she just looks at the floor and doesn't speak. She has on her bright red parka, and the fur of the hood almost obscures her face. About an inch above the hem, on the front and back, are colorful Inuit scenes which her Inuk god-mother has embroidered on the coat.

"Collette! What's up? What's the matter?" Sharla goes over and grabs her arm. *"Tell me."*

"You're gonna be so angry. And I guess I don't blame you."

"What *is* it? I figure it's you who should be mad at *me*."

Collette starts to unzip her parka and kick

off her boots. She's moving very slowly. Sharla can see that there are dark circles under her eyes. *Someone else didn't sleep very well last night.*

"It was my fault," says Collette.

"What was your fault?"

"It was my fault that he called the Bear Patrol. I could have stopped him, but I didn't."

"What on earth are you talking about, Collette? Stopped who?"

"Theo. We were there, watching you. Like two spies. I'm so ashamed. He told me that he was working on his anger. Trying not to get mad about you running around with that tourist. In the truck and in the Complex and walking all over town. With him fixing your hair, and all. He'd seen you get in his truck on the road down to the beach. He was mad and he was scared."

Collette stops and sits down at the kitchen table. She takes the mug of hot chocolate from Sharla and warms her hands on it.

"What did you see?" Sharla asks. "Everything? Him putting out the meat? All that camera equipment in my lap? The bear coming straight at us?"

"Yes," says Collette. "We saw everything. Theo kept muttering, 'They're crazy. *Crazy!*' Then, when the bear got closer to the truck, he said, 'I'm calling the Bear Patrol,' and stood up. I yelled at him, 'Don't you dare do that! She'll be so mad that she'll never speak to you again. If you really like her, *don't do it*.' I told him that the tourist guy —"

"Jake," says Sharla.

". . . that Jake will be leaving on Monday afternoon. That everything would be fine then. He said, 'I'd like her to be *alive* on Monday afternoon.' I said that if he called the Bear Patrol everyone would know about it. That your parents would just about kill you. But he started walking towards the Local Government District office to use their phone. It was like he was sleepwalking or in a trance or something. I stood in front of the door. I could have stopped him. I know I could have. If I hadn't moved, he wouldn't have grabbed me and flung me aside. But with his eyes cold as ice, all he did was say:

'*Get out of my way.* I don't give a shit about her parents or whether they'll be mad. *I'm* mad. Sharla and that idiot are too dumb to honk the horn or drive away. That bear is gonna get them.' And what did I do? I just slid away from the door and let him go in."

Collette sighed, and then went on.

"Sharla, I couldn't believe how fast those Patrol guys came. When we went back to the window, we saw them shooting the bear, and watched you come out and touch the bear and start crying. I felt so awful. About you. About the bear. I wouldn't even speak to Theo afterwards. I just ran out of there and went home."

"Take it easy, Collette," says Sharla. "Both of you missed the most important part. The bear broke the window. A whole lot of him was in that truck, snuffling around and putting out his big paw to get the meat we'd kept in the cab. *I could feel his breath, Collette.* I don't ever want to be that scared again — not in my whole life. I just knew we were going to die, or worse still, be clawed to bits."

Sharla stands up and gets more hot chocolate from the stove.

"We needed that Bear Patrol. And it's OK. The bear's not dead. They just put him to sleep. Last evening, he had his first comfy night in the Bear Jail. He'll be out and free, long before the end of November."

"But your parents . . ."

Sharla takes a breath, and pauses before answering. "I can't do anything about them. They'll find out, I know that. It's gonna be rough, for sure, and they'll likely want to hang Jake up by his thumbs. And I've done so much bad stuff lately that I don't know what they'll decide to do about me — lying, disobeying, getting tossed out of basketball practice, doing lousy work at school, being late all the time, making most of the teachers mad. And Collette . . ."

"Yes?"

"Jake. He's got a *daughter*. A daughter the same age as us. For him to be twenty-eight years old, she'd have had to be born when he was thirteen!"

"Wow!"

"So . . . I thought I was wildly in love with someone who turned out to be an old man. He could be almost the same age as my parents. About forty-two. Anyway, even if he still was twenty-eight, I'd be too mad at him now to think I loved him."

"Why? How come? He was supposed to be so perfect."

Sharla could feel herself blushing. "Well, I thought he was. But he wouldn't honk the horn when the bear attacked the truck. I kept pleading with him, yelling, 'Please! Please!' He told me to shut up. He called me a little fool. He was ready to risk both our lives just so he could get his stupid pictures. He looked at me in such an angry way, like he hated me. And he's got that daughter. I could string him up by the thumbs myself."

Collette grins. "Then I'm not in the dog-house?"

"No. And Collette, thank you for rescuing my books from the snowbank. I'm sorry I was such a turkey. I'd like to slap myself till I turn black and blue."

Collette grins. "Sharla," she says. "I

brought my books. I thought I could maybe help you with your math. Getting caught up and all. You going out with Jake today?"

"No." Sharla is surprised to hear herself laughing. "I resigned from my big job. All this fuss, and all I ever made was fifteen dollars. He's coming out with me and Benjamin, Halloween night, but only because he's got as much right to be on the streets as I do. And Benjamin will be with me. That makes it OK. I guess so, anyway. I hope so."

Collette takes her mug over to the sink and rinses it off. "So we can work for a couple of hours. I have to babysit my sister later on, but we can get a lot done in that time." Collette starts to get her books out of her backpack.

❖❖❖

Two hours later, Sharla knows a lot more about equations than she did when she got up that morning. Collette has just left, and Sharla leans back on the kitchen counter, feeling peaceful and virtuous about having finished her math homework so early on the weekend. All she has left to do is some literature stuff for Mrs. Joyce — a poem by Matthew Arnold, another of Mrs. J's literary heroes. That can wait until tonight. Right now, she'd like to go out and feel some of that wind on her face — even though it's eighteen below zero. With the wind-chill factor, that makes it close to minus thirty-nine. That's OK. It may blow some of the fuzziness out of her head. Maybe she'll go down to the Northern Images store and covet the soapstone ptarmigan for a few minutes. They don't mind if you go in there to admire the stuff, even if you can't buy anything. Or she could check out the Bay from the Complex window, to see if it's closer to being frozen over. No. She isn't ready to look at that beach again. Not yet.

She puts on her warm parka and mitts, and leaves the house. Benjamin will be at Steven's all afternoon, so she's free to go wherever she wants, and to be gone as long as she chooses.

Her first stop is the Arctic Trading

Company, where she admires all the clothes and jewelry she can't afford to buy. If she was rich like that tourist who's busy paying for a pair of beaded moccasins, she'd buy that suede vest with the fringes. The color would be perfect with her sandy hair, and it'd look cool with her black turtle-neck T-shirt. Then she goes over to the Tundra Buggy office, and looks at the polar bear quilts. She wants one so badly — now, more than ever. The quilts have squares with three overlaid polar bears appliqued on every one. Sharla thinks she'd look forward all day to going to bed if she knew she could crawl under one of those each night.

Then, with the wind at her back, she trudges over to Northern Images — saved till the last, because it contains the ptarmigan.

As soon as she opens the door, Sharla has a sense of something being wrong. Maybe it's the serious way the owner is looking at her — without her usual smile. The ptarmigan is always at the corner of the table, on the edge. In spite of a sign that asks customers not to touch the works of art, the clerk always lets her run her index finger over his smooth surface. She knows how much Sharla loves him, and how careful she is. Now Sharla sees what's wrong. He's gone. There's just a sad little bare space where he used to be.

The clerk comes up to Sharla. "I'm sorry," she says, her eyes troubled. "We sold it this morning to a tourist. Two of them came in — a man and a woman — and the woman bought it. We had to sell it, Sharla. We're not a museum. We're a store, a business. But I'm sorry all the same."

While I was doing math, some damn tourist came in with her damn husband and her damn money, and stole my ptarmigan.

"That's OK," she says. But it isn't OK at all. She knows that she couldn't expect the store not to sell that bird just so she could come in once a week and slide her finger over his back. But he'd been there for so long that she'd begun to feel he was going to be on that table forever.

She leaves the store feeling tired and slow, as though all the energy has been zapped right out of her. As she passes the grocery store, she meets Theo coming out with a bag of food.

"Hi," she says.

"Hi." Then, "I'm sorry."

"For what?"

"For spoiling your party. For killing the bear. For getting mad at someone who wasn't doing anything all that wrong."

Sharla grins at him. "You didn't spoil my party. You probably saved my life. And you didn't kill the bear, and neither did anyone else. They just put him to sleep — very fast. And about Jake. He *was* doing something wrong."

Theo's brows are drawn together. "What, for instance?"

"For instance, he was risking both our lives and acting like a five-year-old. So was I, but I'm a lot closer to that age than he is." She laughs. Then she tells him the whole story. "Now I'm mad at him," she says, "and by Monday night, when my parents will have heard all about it from about fifty inhabitants of Churchill, I expect I'll be mad at a whole lot of other people, too."

Theo peers into the bag he's carrying. "Let's go up to the Complex and warm up," he says. "If we stand out here any longer, all my groceries are going to freeze solid. I bought some hamburger for supper, and I don't want to have to thaw it out before I cook it. And lettuce. That's probably wrecked already." He shifts the groceries to one arm, and takes her hand as they walk up the street.

She hasn't thought before about Theo and food. With his mother gone and his father drunk half the time, who's been cooking their meals for the last five years? Probably Theo. He must have had to learn to cook in a heck of a hurry. She thinks about Theo's mother and her many unanswered letters to him. She figures it will probably take more than Outreach Services to make Theo able to forgive her. It makes Sharla sad, just thinking about that. Sad for Theo. And sad for his mother, too. It must be awful to be sorry, and to find out that no one believes you or even cares.

Up at the Complex, she discovers that she's ready to look out the window after all. The slob ice is now gathered on the edge of the beach and far out over the water, breathing in and out with the swell of the sea. But there are no waves breaking. Sharla knows she's seen the last of them until spring. She's already been told that there are often giant ice floes in the water as late as July 1st, when they hold their famous Polar Bear Dip.

"You'll like it when it's completely frozen," says Theo. "Just wait. You'll see."

She ignores that. "I hope they got all the meat we put out yesterday. Jake put it in three places. I was too strung out to notice if they picked all of it up."

"Well," says Theo, "if they didn't, we may have an interesting Halloween night tomorrow. The Bear Patrol had better stay awake and make sure their searchlights are working."

❖❖❖

That evening, after Benjamin is in bed, Sharla opens her English literature textbook.

So it's Matthew Arnold, tonight. Whoever he is. Or was. And the poem is "Dover Beach." She's supposed to know that poem inside out by Monday morning. Not memorize it; just know and understand it from start to finish. Just. She sighs. Then she starts to read:

> The sea is calm tonight,
> The tide is full . . .

and then, later:

> Listen! You hear the grating roar
> Of pebbles which the waves draw back,
>   and fling,
> At their return, up the high strand,
> Begin and cease, and then begin again.

and finally:

> Ah, love, let us be true
> To one another! for the world which
>   seems
> To lie before us like a land of dreams,
> So various, so beautiful, so new,
> Hath really neither joy, nor love, nor
>   light,

> *Nor certitude, nor peace, nor help for*
>   *pain;*
> *And we are here as on a darkling plain,*
> *Swept with confused alarms of struggle*
>   *and flight,*
> *Where ignorant armies clash by night.*

Sharla leans back against the sofa cushions and closes her eyes. *"Ah, love, let us be true to one another."* Why is she thinking about Theo? What kind of person is she, anyway? Four months ago (which seems like a hundred years back) her idol was Rich Harrigan in Ottawa. Five days ago, Mr. Kent had been her knight in shining armour. Well, he sort of still is, but only as a part of her whole basketball dream. Then she switched channels and started loving Jake so hard that she'd begun working out complicated arithmetic about how old he'd be when she was forty. She was wanting to *marry* him. And now she's sitting here, reading this incredibly beautiful and sad poem, and thinking about Theo. Also thinking that she doesn't ever want to live any place where there is no sea.

Well, she'll go to bed now, and see who'll be the hero tonight in her nightime day-dreams. That should tell her something.

CHAPTER TEN

When Sharla wakes up on October 31st, she lies still for a while and stares up at the ceiling. It's much colder. This she knows without going to look at the thermometer. Her nose feels cold — even her ears. She arranges her long hair so that it covers her ears, and rubs her nose with her middle finger. With that wind, she thinks, it could be close to forty-five below zero out there. What a drag. This evening, the kids will have to cover up their costumes with so many hats and scarves that they won't look like costumes any more.

Halloween night. She knows you aren't supposed to be interested in Halloween when you're fifteen. But she is. Some of the kids in her class would laugh themselves silly if they knew that it was her favorite festival of the whole year. All those jack-o'-lanterns leering at you from the dark windows. Little kids racing from house to house, their plastic bags of candy bumping up against their knees. Masks. Scary costumes. She's always loved it. It makes her remember all sorts of ways in which it was fun to be a kid.

But here, in Churchill, it could be even more interesting than in other places. Where else would there be a whole army of people out there to protect the kids? Where else would that be needed? In spite of her close call with the bear two days ago, Sharla finds that something inside her is thrilled by the idea of a Halloween night that could be genuinely dangerous. All the children will be carrying food — something that is an open invitation to a bear. With the Bay almost frozen over, the bears are steadily

moving up from the area south of Churchill
— walking close to shore so that they can
leave the land and move out onto the ice as
soon as it's ready to hold them.

Tonight, all around the perimeter of the
town, trucks and vans will be stationed,
training their searchlights out onto the beach
and rocks and tundra, ready to intercept
any bear who might try to approach the
community. There will be people from
Natural Resources, the RCMP, the fire
department. And all evening long, Bear
Patrol cars will be cruising up and down the
Churchill streets, making sure that no bear
has slipped by their watchful eyes.

Sharla smiles at the ceiling. This is pretty
intriguing stuff. And she doesn't have to
stay at home and pretend that she's too old
for such foolishness. Because she's officially
babysitting, she'll have to go out with
Benjamin and his friend Steven, accompany-
ing them on their rounds.

She leaps out of bed and goes down to
turn up the heat. Inside his room, Benjamin
is busy working on his pirate costume,

oblivious to the cold. Sharla decides she'll get dressed up, too. A witch's outfit will be easy to put together. She can make the pointed hat out of a sheet of that black bristol board that she's seen in the store-room, and her mother has some old curtains that have a pattern on one side but are plain black on the other — if she can just find them among the packing boxes. She can put one of them over her coat, for a voluminous cape. She can black out two of her teeth, and also carry the kitchen broom. Pretty simple and pretty perfect.

All this can be prepared this afternoon, but first she wants to check out the Bay. She grabs a piece of cheese and a slice of bread, wolfing it all down with a glass of milk.

"Did you eat your breakfast?" she calls out to Benjamin.

"No! I'm not hungry."

"Well, get out here and eat something!"

"Why?" he shouts.

"Because I say so!" she yells back.

She grins to herself. *If Mom dropped dead this afternoon, and I was left to look after*

Benjamin, I'd start sounding exactly like her within twenty-four hours.

❖

Over at the Complex, Sharla climbs up to the second floor and walks past the Launching Pad, past the pictures of the former inhabitants of the area, past the benches, and over to the window.

It's gone. The water is gone. As far as the eye can see, the Bay is white with ice and blowing snow. The air is clear, and the sky a cloudless blue. Someone once told her that Churchill can get colder than certain areas of the high Arctic.

When Sharla looks out that window, she feels as though she *is* in the high Arctic. In spite of the wind and the snow skimming off the ice surface, there is an atmosphere of stillness and silence, and of something closing in. "The winter has closed in," she says aloud, and finds that the idea appeals to her. *By May, I may be feeling differently,* she thinks, but right now, it's OK. She likes that experience of limitless white. She loves the hugeness of the sky which for some reason she doesn't understand, looks bigger than it did yesterday. She feels stunned by its blueness and by the extreme whiteness of the Bay.

And the bears, she thinks, will now come into their own. Maybe in some places the ice is already strong enough to hold them, but if not today, then very soon. They'll come up the coast, moving with their deliberate and confident gait, delicately and slowly placing one foot after the other, and they'll move off onto the ice, into the blowing snow. Warm under their layers of fat and fur, they'll spend their time hunting and wandering, sleeping and eating, enjoying the long northern winter. They'll be where they really belong. Some wheel or other will have come full circle.

❖

That afternoon, Sharla is able to assemble and construct her witch's costume. She helps Benjamin with his eye-patch — necessary for every self-respecting pirate — and they tie his red kerchief around his head at various angles, to find which way makes him look most fierce. As it gets closer and closer to darkness, she paints whiskers on his face with her eyeliner. On her own face she draws freckles, a grim pair of lines between her eyebrows, and dark red lipstick. The cape will be great over her jacket, and can be held in place by that giant safety pin she's just seen among some old baby equipment in the storeroom. For their candy bags, she digs out a couple of shabby old pillowcases from the bathroom cupboard.

Sharla hands Benjamin an apple and some nuts. "Better eat something healthy," she says. "We'll be having candy and popcorn for supper."

Then Steven arrives — a fat bumblebee in a huge striped black and yellow costume, which fits over all his outer clothes. Two pipe-cleaner antennae stick out of his woolen toque, and his earmuffs make him look even more like a bumblebee.

At six o'clock, they leave the house. There, on the corner, is Jake — waiting. Someone must have lent him a parka, because he looks almost warm enough to survive the next few hours. It's minus twenty-four with a driving wind, which makes it much, much colder; more like forty-eight below.

"Hi, Jake," says Sharla.

"Hi," he says. "Still mad?"

"Yes," she says, "but not enough to leave you stranded on Halloween night. Besides, I'm not so much mad as I'm just sort of switched off."

"Switched off?"

"Yeah. Tuned out."

He looks puzzled, but he doesn't waste time with questions about that. He has other more important things to ask.

"Where do I find the people who've set themselves up to defend the town?" he says mockingly, but only slightly so. After all, two days earlier, he'd been sharing the front seat of a truck with a polar bear.

Steven answers the question. "Over at the north end of the Complex, in their van, with their searchlights."

"Dressed in their orange suits," adds

Sharla. "Or so they tell me. It'd make a pretty sharp picture. That and the search-lights sweeping the beach for intruders."

"The Mounties are watching from near Caribou Hall," puts in Steven, "and the fire department truck is at the far end of town, close to the Backroad."

"Thanks," says Jake. "I'll be off as soon as I get a few shots on this street. I've got 1600 ASA film in one of my cameras. If the thing doesn't jam in this temperature, the pictures should be terrific."

It's very dark now, with the orange pumpkin faces eerie against the blackness. The snow is bright beneath the small figures darting from house to house — clowns, bur-glars, soldiers, goblins, angels with their wings pinned to their parkas and garlands of paper flowers on top of their hoods. Jake's camera is clicking away as he changes position to shoot the scene from different angles. He also takes many shots of the tall witch in her cardboard hat. Sharla tries not to notice, and tells herself that she doesn't care, but at one point, she can't resist turning to him and grinning her gap-toothed smile.

Click, click. He takes two more shots. Then he lowers the camera and speaks to her. "I'm sorry about Friday. I was irresponsible, and I know it."

"Yes," she says. "I know. But not just irresponsible. Also rude and nasty. You told me to shut up. And called me a little fool. Yelled at me. That's how come I tuned out."

"I still don't understand what you mean by 'tuned out'."

"I get too much of that nasty stuff at home. My parents are mad a lot of the time — at each other and at us kids. They're going through a bad time, but they shouldn't take it out on us. Teachers bug me too. I seem to be stirring up a lot of mud these days. Which makes me angry. Often. Too often. So it's a big thing for me when I meet someone who acts like I'm OK. Someone with kind eyes. I'm always looking for kind eyes."

"And . . .?"

"You seemed like that. You trusted me to work for you, and I thought you had kind eyes. So I was really happy, and I was fond of you. Then you did all those stupid things — baiting a bear, and acting like a sitting duck so that he could smash the window and get in the truck. And calling me names and looking so full of hate when I yelled at you to honk the horn. So I tuned out. I switched off."

"Switched off what? When I was younger, switching off meant something else."

"Switched off the liking. It's what I do if someone I care about hurts me. I just can't waste my valuable energy liking someone I can't trust." Then she pauses. "Maybe that's what your daughter feels when she says you think pictures are more important than people. You told me about that as if it was some sort of a joke. But I didn't find it funny."

"But I'm sorry," says Jake. "Doesn't that make the whole thing OK? Doesn't that change anything?"

Sharla looks at Jake's handsome face and his kind eyes. In spite of everything, it makes her heart beat faster just to look at him. "Up to a point, yes," she says. "But not completely. It takes some of the anger out of me, which is good. But I'm still switched off. That's the way I am. It's my armour. Like the knights in Tennyson's poems. It keeps them from being pierced to the heart." *Am I really doing this? Using old Tennyson to illustrate how I'm feeling?*

But suddenly Sharla realizes that they've been standing in one place, while Steven and Benjamin have moved on. At almost the same moment, she can hear in the far distance someone's voice calling, "Bear!" Over by the RCMP truck, she can see the searchlights go on. The air is full of questions, shouts, exclamations: "Who saw the bear?" "Where is it?" "Get Johnny fast, and take him home!" "Someone's sighted a bear on the beach!" "Hey, guys! Bears! Get inside!"

"Jake!" says Sharla, her voice hoarse. "Benjamin and Steven are gone!"

"Oh my God!" breathes Jake. "I've gotta get back there to the Patrol van and see what's going on! This is the chance of a lifetime!"

Sharla stares at him. "You didn't even

hear what I said!" she cries, her voice rising, her breath coming fast. "Steven and Benjamin are *gone*, and there's *a bear* out there someplace!"

"I won't be away more than fifteen minutes," he says, already stuffing his gear into his bag. "I'll be back as soon as I check out the situation and get the pictures. I promise. Then we'll find the boys. Some people wait forever and never get a chance like this. I can't believe I'm this lucky!" There's a kind of glassy brightness in his eyes which makes Sharla think of last Friday on the beach. *He can't see anything out of those eyes. He's already somewhere else. He said he was sorry, but no one ever told him what that word really means.* She watches him as he races up La Verendrye Avenue in the direction of the Complex.

But now, she's doing her own racing. Up and down the streets she runs in the piercing cold, calling, calling, "Steven! Benjamin! Answer me!" But no one replies. The streets are becoming more and more deserted. The goblins and clowns and fairies have disappeared into their own houses, herded in by terrified parents. But Sharla keeps running and calling, running and calling: "Benjamin! Steven! *Please!*" As time passes, she becomes more and more frightened, and she's so tired that she feels as though her lungs are going to burst in the frigid air. She struggles up and down almost every street in the neighborhood, the wind sometimes in her face, sometimes at her back.

Finally, she has to stop for a moment to catch her breath, and she can hear herself sobbing out loud, unable to control her panic. As she stands there, struggling for air, she looks in the direction of her own house. *The lights are on. They're all right.* As she runs again in that direction, her relief is enormous. But it turns almost immediately into anger, and by the time she reaches the house, she can no longer contain it. She opens the door and yells.

"Why didn't you *stay* with me? Why didn't you tell me where you were *going?* I've been so *scared!* How could you *do* this to me?"

She picks up a jar that is sitting on the kitchen counter, and throws it at the opposite wall. It breaks into a thousand pieces. Then she sits down on the floor and cries out loud, the way a tiny child does, in noisy, racking sobs.

Benjamin and Steven stand there, open-mouthed.

"Listen, Sharla," Benjamin says. "I'm real sorry you were scared about us. But you were with that Jake guy. You just went on and on, talking and talking. So we couldn't wait. The candy might all be gone."

"The *candy* might all be gone!"

"Yeah. And then when they started yelling about a bear, we did what Mom told us to do. We hot-footed it straight home and went in and shut the door."

Sharla is breathing more normally now. She lets out a long sigh, and wipes her face with the back of her sleeve. Her fake freckles are all running together, and her witch's hat is askew. She pushes it to the back of her head and shuts her eyes. Can anyone be this tired without dying?

There's a knock at the door. Benjamin goes to open it, but Jake is already inside the kitchen.

"Oh, good!" he says cheerfully. "Everyone's safe!"

Sharla doesn't answer him. She can't trust her voice yet to get out the things she's longing to say.

"I got some terrific shots!" He's so excited that his voice isn't quite steady. "There actually was a bear. They tranquilized him, like on Friday. You should have seen those orange suits against the black night, and then against the white sea. And the bear! The orange and the black and the white — a photographer's dream, all of it. And there'll be a new visitor at the Polar Bear Jail tonight!" He laughs. Then he stops.

Sharla is just looking at him, a long, cold, level look.

"Hey! Sharla! Don't look like that! I ran all the way back in all that wind. I know it was more than fifteen minutes, but what's the sweat? You're all OK."

Sharla takes a long, deep breath. She

hopes she can get her speech out without her voice cracking or the tears starting up again. She wishes she was standing up, and that she didn't have to say all this with a smeared face and blacked-out teeth.

"Jake," she says, and her voice is both quiet and steady, "I want you to take all your billion-dollar camera equipment, and I want you to get out of my house."

Sharla leans her head back against the wall for a moment and closes her eyes. She takes another long breath, and feels a tear squeeze through her lids. But she finds that she can continue her speech.

"And when you go back to New York City," she says, "I want you to go right up to your daughter's room. I want you to sit down on the edge of her bed, and maybe take her hand. Then I want you to ask her this question: 'What did you mean when you said that I liked my pictures more than I liked people?' Then, if she finds it too hard to give you an answer, write to me and ask me the same question. I'll be very happy to tell you. Our Post Office Box is 203."

Jake starts to speak. But Sharla hasn't finished yet.

"Or maybe," she continues, "if you think really hard, you'll be able to come up with the answer yourself. Now — get out!"

❖❖

After Jake has left, Sharla looks up and sees that Benjamin is already starting to sweep up the broken glass. Steven is holding the dustpan.

"No, guys," she says, as she staggers to her feet. "This one's on me. It's me who threw it. Sorry I blew my top."

Then she takes the broom and works on the floor until there isn't a single piece of glass left anywhere. After that, all three of them sit down and have candy and hot chocolate for their supper. Sharla rolls her eyes to the ceiling. "Lovely, lovely junk food," she says. They won't be able to have a meal like this again for a long time. Tomorrow, their parents are coming home.

CHAPTER ELEVEN

Sharla gets up long before dawn to neat up the house. There'll be enough ammunition coming her way without adding a messy house and dirty dishes to the list of her other sins. She's weary, but she's so nervous about her parents' reactions to her crazy behavior during their absence, that her adrenalin is pumping hard, filling her with another kind of energy. Rushing around the house helps to center her — washing dishes, mopping the grungy linoleum, picking up the dozens of things she's left lying around on the floor, the tables, the counters. By the time she and

Benjamin leave for school, she feels more or less calm.

"Sure was fun last night!" pants Benjamin as he rushes to catch up with her long-legged stride. He's overslept and missed the bus. "Ever great that a bear came to town, on Halloween. But I wish I'd seen him!"

"Huh!" comments Sharla. She feels as though she's seen enough bears to last her for quite a while. And no. She doesn't think last night was fun. At all.

It's another clear day, and beyond the town, the sun, still low in the sky, is catching the edges of the hummocks of the tundra, and lighting up the little glacial ponds that dot the landscape. The snow blows off the slippery lakes, leaving them so smooth and shiny that they look as though the water hasn't frozen over yet.

School's sort of OK. She's done her homework, and she's done it well. She enjoys the discussion of "Dover Beach," and even throws in the odd comment herself. "I think life's a lot like those last two lines," she says.

Mrs. Joyce seems both amazed and

pleased by this contribution from a student who's done little except frown at her for two months. "Who do you think the 'ignorant armies' are, Sharla?" she asks. "Who's the poem talking about?"

"Most of us, I guess," says Sharla. "Parents, politicians, tourists, gangsters . . . and even us kids. Maybe especially us kids — 'full of confused alarms of struggle and flight.' That sounds like a lot of stuff I can relate to."

Later, Sharla is the last one to leave the classroom at noon. She smiles at Mrs. Joyce as she comes abreast of her desk. "I like that poem," she says.

"I know you do, Sharla," says Mrs. Joyce. "That's probably because it says something that strikes a chord in you. I know it's hard to like a poem if there's nothing in it that reaches your own thinking or experience."

"Like that Wordsworth poem about the daffodils," grins Sharla. "Not something we know much about in Churchill. 'Ten thousand saw I at a glance, / Tossing their heads in sprightly dance.' *Sheesh!*"

"But you've seen them. There must be a lot of daffodils sprinkled in among all those tulips in Ottawa. You can remember them. You can think of the poem in terms of daffodils that *were*, or maybe *will be*. Not just the fact that they don't grow easily in Churchill. Or maybe you just have to resign yourself to the fact that you don't like the poem."

"You mean that's OK?"

Mrs. Joyce laughs. "Of course it's OK. You can't very well be blamed for something over which you have no control. I love that poem, and it's also a part of my job to present it to you. I put the food on your plate, and you're supposed to eat it. But I can't force you to enjoy the meal. Still . . . who can tell? Sometime later on, you may think about it and feel differently. You never know."

Like my armour, Tennyson's armour, my protection from being hurt. From being pierced to the heart. "No," says Sharla, as she leaves the room. "You never know."

Sharla spends her spare period with

Collette, and tells her about Halloween and her experience with Jake.

"What a turkey!" says Collette.

Sharla nods. "Yeah. But even while I was hating him last night, I was seeing how beautiful he looked. I guess I'm not quite as switched off as I think I am."

"Good thing for you that he's leaving today," says Collette. "How's he going?"

"Flying. To Winnipeg, and then on to the States."

"And your mom and dad?"

"They're coming back in on the plane that'll take him out. I can hardly wait for the explosion that's going to happen when they find out what's been going on the last few days. I figure by the time I get home this afternoon, they'll know everything. News travels fast in a small town. I learned that last week." She screws up her face. "I can hardly wait."

At noon, Sharla eats her lunch at the Complex Launching Pad. Theo leaves a group of his friends and comes over to sit beside her.

"How's it going?" he asks. "You look sort of calmed down or something. Almost peaceful. On you, it looks good." He grins.

Sharla laughs. "Peaceful? More like exhausted. You should have seen me last night, when I was throwing things around."

"Like what?"

"A giant glass pickle jar. Minus the pickles. You can't believe how many pieces of glass a broken pickle jar can generate."

Theo guffaws. "Oh yes, I can. I've swept up a lot of broken glass in my time, too."

"But you seem to be kind of together now. It must be nice to have so many things worked out. You're getting to be a regular marshmallow." Sharla laughs again.

"Believe me, I'm no marshmallow. Sometimes I feel like a walking timebomb. Look how I reacted when Jake was in the picture. I was mad just because he was *with* you. Just because he was *employing* you. That's sick, and I knew it."

"Why sick? Just sounds a little bit jealous to me."

"Yeah. But there's jealous and jealous. At

Outreach they told me that lots of abused kids end up wanting to abuse other people, sometimes even their own children. So you really have to watch it when you feel an unreasonable anger rising in yourself — like when you're angry at someone who hasn't really done anything wrong. You need to learn how to defuse the bomb before it explodes."

"But how? I sure wasn't doing much defusing last night."

"Well, I do a lot of physical stuff, like playing hockey or soccer or jogging, or something. Hockey's best, because you're slamming a puck around and going really fast. And you get concentrating on the game and forget your anger for a while."

"Great time for me to be shut out of the gym!" says Sharla, grinning. "And nobody's going to get me out jogging in this weather. I sure don't know what I'll do if Mom or Dad start tossing grenades at me the minute I get in the house. And knowing I deserve a lot of it probably isn't going to help me one bit."

"Call me," says Theo. "I'll come over to your house and collect you. Then we can try to walk it off. Or you could go over to Outreach and spill your beans. Talking about it helps. Believe me."

Then he laughs. "I think I'm nagging you," he says.

"You are," says Sharla. But she likes being here with him. He knows about her wheels, and understands the way they turn. Besides, she likes his shaggy hair and big strong hands. And he doesn't look one bit rosy-cheeked. Or pimply. Or untested.

Sharla is silent for a while, as she thinks about all those things. Then she looks at Theo and says, "You know when Collette was barring the LGD door to keep you from calling the Bear Patrol? She said that you'd never have pushed her aside if she'd stayed there. Is that true?"

Theo laughs. "Uh-uh. If she'd stayed there, I was wild enough to pick her up and throw her clear across the Complex. I would've at least grabbed her and yanked her out of the doorway. She'd have had bruises on her arm for a week."

"Well, I'm sure glad you called them. No way was I wanting to be that bear's breakfast."

When they go over to look out the big window, they can see that a storm is gathering. The snow on the ice is swirling around like an evil spell. The sun has disappeared, and dark clouds are racing across the sky. They hear the sound of a plane's engines overhead.

"Good thing the plane got out before the storm started," says Theo.

"Yes," says Sharla. *Better than you realize. Jake is on that plane. He's gone.* Then she frowns. *And my parents are back.*

Before classes start, Sharla goes down to the library to borrow a book for a geography assignment. "Anything else I can do for you?" asks Mrs. Cole, giving her the book.

"No thanks," says Sharla. And then: "Well . . . maybe. Do you have any stuff by that Arnold guy? The poet. Matthew. Matthew Arnold. Do you?"

Mrs. Cole goes off to search for a volume,

checks it out, and hands it to Sharla. She smiles. "Friend of yours?"

"Yes," says Sharla.

⚜

As the afternoon passes, Sharla finds it more and more difficult to concentrate. What will her parents say or do? Mr. Lovitt tells the class that he's been talking about the European feudal system so that he can link it to the Seigneurial System of old Quebec, but she doesn't even hear him. She makes five mistakes on a spot test in math, because she isn't focused enough to think carefully.

When school is over, Sharla looks long-ingly at the group that's filing into the gym for basketball practice. She visualizes herself dribbling the ball down the court, sinking a basket, running back, intercepting, scoring another two points. She watches from the doorway, close to tears. Mr. Kent passes her as he enters the gym, and then turns back to speak to her, his eyes noticeably kind.

"Hang in there, Sharla," he says. "Believe it or not, time will pass. In about eighteen days, you'll be back in there." Then his eyes change, and his face becomes stern. "But make sure you pull up your socks. You don't *need* to be late for school so often. And you're a smart kid. You can get good grades, if you really try. If by any chance you're still able to make it onto the school team, remember this: I won't tolerate it if one of my players gets banned from the gym, even for a short time. So — *watch it*."

Then he puts his hand on her shoulder and says, "I realize that this is rough for you. I'm sorry. But I also know you can turn things around if you really try."

❖

Sharla spends much of the afternoon with Collette, but she knows she can't put off facing her parents forever. As she walks home, she takes pleasure in the gathering storm. The wind is slamming so hard against her body that it's almost difficult to stay upright. *Maybe this is where I belong — me and all my turbulent feelings. Instead of quiet old, serene old, dignified old Ottawa, with the politicians and diplomats gliding to and fro in their limousines, looking after the affairs of the nation. Ottawa seems like a foreign land to me now.* She looks back to the Health Centre, where the Outreach Services have their offices. "I think I'm almost ready for that now," she whispers, as she presses her scarf closer to her face. "After a couple of interesting hours with my parents, I may want to make an emergency appointment."

But when she opens the door to her house, her mother is all smiles. She looks rested and happy, after her time in Thompson. *A very pretty chick* are the words that ring in Sharla's head.

"How was Halloween night?" asks her mom. Sharla looks across the kitchen at Benjamin, who is spreading a slice of bread with peanut butter and jam. He glances up at her and grins. He also squeezes his face into a wink. He hasn't told. She shoots him a grateful look.

"It was fine," says Sharla. "Benjamin was a great pirate, and I was a pretty good witch. With teeth missing. Lots of candy, which we had for supper, instead of that healthy stuff you left for us in the freezer."

"I hear there was a bear down behind the Complex," says her mother, as she tosses a salad in the big wooden bowl.

"Yeah. In school today they said he weighed seven hundred pounds. Pretty big. And Benjamin knew exactly what to do. He raced home and shut the door. You should be proud of him."

But not of me. Standing on a street corner and forgetting all about him. Talking to the forbidden Jake.

Obviously her mother hasn't yet heard about the bear incident on Friday. *But she will, that's for sure — tomorrow, the next day, or the next.* And when she asks questions about it, or when her father asks, Sharla will have to tell exactly what happened. She wonders if it's the same as a lie to leave out some details of what happened on Halloween night. She hopes not, but maybe it is. She can't decide. She knows that Benjamin won't betray her. But Steven might tell his mother. He was another witness to the flying pickle jar. And to other things.

Sharla sighs. "How was Thompson?"

"Thompson was great. We looked into a job there for your father, but it was filled. We went to a movie and ate in restaurants. We spent a lot of money, but it was OK because I had my pay from the Tundra Inn."

"Does that make it OK with Dad?"

"Well, it certainly made it better. Don't worry. He'll get used to it."

"What about the house?"

"We checked with the real estate person and the lawyer, but it's still not sold. We brought the price down a bit, so maybe that'll make a difference. Perhaps it may take a while, but when it's sold, our life will be a whole lot easier."

"And Dad?"

"Oh, you know. Pretty depressed and edgy, although he seemed a lot happier when we were away. It was getting back here that was hard. Life is a rocky road for him, right now."

"And for all of us."

"Yes. But hardest of all for him.

Remember, he had this big job with a fat salary which he thought would be his forever. So he tossed his money around as though he owned the Mint. Big house — bigger than we needed. Two cars. Golf club fees, clothes, the trips we took, restaurants, concerts, sports equipment. Anything he wanted, he bought. Even *with* a job, that's a shortcut to getting into debt. But if you lose your job, it becomes a catastrophe. He knows all that now. In the old days, he refused to live any other way. So now he feels guilty. I know it's hard for us, too. But at least we don't have to feel that it's all our fault. It must be awful to have to face your own guilt."

You may not have to feel guilty, but I know all about it. "Where is he right now?"

"Just his luck. He's on evening shift tonight."

Suddenly Sharla finds herself saying, "He should go over to Outreach Services and see if they can give him some help. I'm going myself on Wednesday."

"*You*? You seem pretty OK to me. Anyway, a lot better than a while back."

Another surprise: Sharla adds, "Mr. Lovitt says that things always get a little bit better before people start working on the big improvements. He was talking about the French Revolution, but I'm starting to think he was talking about the whole human race."

❖❖

Later that evening, Sharla thinks about the way nothing has been resolved. Her parents don't yet know about the bear-baiting incident, her visit to the principal, her disobedience about Jake, her behavior on Halloween night. Some of it they may never find out. But most of it they'll hear about within a day or two. Probably tomorrow. Wednesday will be an excellent day for going to Outreach.

Her mother knocks at her bedroom door. She comes in, holding a parcel. "A woman just left this," she says. "For you." Then, when Sharla makes no move to open the parcel, she leaves the room, closing the door quietly behind her.

There's a note with the package, but

Sharla opens the box first. It's gift-wrapped. There, lying in a nest of tissue paper, is her soapstone ptarmigan. Quickly, Sharla rips open the note. It says:

Dear Sharla:
Here is your ptarmigan. Someone will deliver it to you after I'm gone. A woman at the Tundra Inn bought it, but this morning I told her that I had to have it, and that if she didn't sell it to me I thought I might steal it from her — at gun-point. So she sold it to me (scared, I guess), and went back to the store and bought a walrus, instead. She seems to like it almost as much. I hope so.

I also hope that this gift will convince you that I've started asking myself the question you wanted me to ask my daughter. I've asked it of myself before, but I've always come up with the wrong answers. Maybe you helped me to look in different places for the right one. That was your gift to me. This is mine to you.

Gratefully,
Jake

Sharla sits for a long time on the edge of her bed, holding the ptarmigan. She feels its fat stone body in her hands, and runs her fingers over its smooth head and back. *It's mine, forever.* No matter what the next few days or months may bring, she knows that she now possesses a truly unique and beautiful thing. She also moves her hand across the letter, as though caressing it — not because of any love for Jake, but because of some other important thing that she can't quite identify — not yet, anyway. But she knows she feels happy. And she realizes that although her original feelings for Jake have vanished, she is once more tuned in, switched on. He's a person to her again, one for whom she feels a fondness and to whom she is grateful, even though she has no idea why. *Not just the ptarmigan. Something else.*

Sharla gets up off the bed and walks to the window, drawing aside the blue curtains. The storm has passed, and the sky is clear, the air still. The lights of the neighboring houses are out, and the night is dark. But in front of her and above, the Northern Lights are shifting and swimming in the sky, luminous, compelling. She saw them once before in Nova Scotia during July. They had filled the sky — grey-white streamers of light, constantly moving among the stars, with a silent, immaculate grace. But this is Churchill, Manitoba, and it's the first of November. Nothing has prepared her for the color and the vividness of what she is seeing. She stands there for a long time, scarcely breathing. *Where have I been during the past weeks? How could I have failed to witness such a miracle? Trapped inside my own head, with the blinds pulled tightly down.*

When she finally stops watching and closes the curtains, she lies in her bed and contemplates the dark ceiling. *Tomorrow I'm going to ask Theo if he'll come with me to the Complex while I go down the polar bear slide. I'll also show him my ptarmigan, and hope that he'll understand how it got to be mine.*

Sharla thinks about the sky outside her window, dancing in the silent night.

"This is my place," she says, and falls asleep.